TO HELL AND BACK

TO HELL AND BACK

JED & JODIE DESPERADOS
BOOK 1

ASH LINGAM

WISE WOLF
BOOKS

WISE WOLF BOOKS
An Imprint of Wolfpack Publishing
wisewolfbooks.com
1707 E. Diana Street
Tampa, FL 33610

Paperback ISBN 978-1-965596-47-0
eBook ISBN 978-1-965596-46-3

Esta novela está dedicado a mi amigo, Tama. Amistades tan largas son de oro, tío.

"And sometimes when I lay with him, I'd look into his face, and he'd look so calm and peaceful there with all the hate erased. He wasn't hearing dying groans or hearing women cry. He wasn't seeing bloody ground or the flames that licked the sky. He'd sleep in peace, and it was me who'd wonder how and why."

Kate Quantrill
Wife of Captain William Quantrill

TO HELL AND BACK

PREFACE

When the American Civil War ended on April 9, 1865, many returned to burned-out homes and lost families. Others didn't agree with the outcome of the conflict. Some of these men drifted south for Texas, and others weren't ready to give up the fight. Many were genuine in their political efforts, and others did it for profit. Many were lost souls like a Confederate soldier by the name of Corporal Jedidiah Coal. As the war progressed, he found himself riding with the notorious William Quantrill and his men by no choice of his own.

Jed was a remarkable shot with a pistol and rifle, a skill he learned as a young boy. Already in his late twenties, he was obliged to sign up to resist the Union and protect the South. Captain William Quantrill saw him on the target range with the new enlistments and snatched him up immediately. The captain claimed Jed was a better shot than any marksman in his regiment and sent him to train as a sniper. He was immediately assigned to the Black Flag Missouri Raiders, who many would argue to be the most brutal men in the ranks of the Confederacy. Just the same, he was thrown into the fray with no introduction, and nobody escaped the effects—not even a simple farmer.

Jodi Goodnight was the niece of a famous Texas rancher. She was born and raised on the back of a horse. By the time she was ten, she could outride and rope better than half the wranglers on her father's ranch. The year of her father's sudden death was the same year the Civil War ended. Most of their cattle had been sold to the Rebel Army. After the war, Confederate currency was worthless.

Jodi found herself on her own and had to learn how to defend herself. By age twenty-two—after long hours of hard work—she could draw and shoot the wings off a fly at forty feet.

For Jodi, the war seemed far from Waco, Texas, but the locals felt the repercussions just the same. She saw how things got worse when the war ended. Little by little, she reduced the number of ranch hands because of lack of funds. Soon, the bank foreclosed, and she lost everything.

By January of 1866, the paths of both young Americans turned and not by their own choice. It was a stroke of fate when their worlds collided. Some would go as far as to call it their destiny.

PROLOGUE

SIX YEARS BEFORE AMERICA WAS DIVIDED BY THE outbreak of the Civil War, the border between Missouri and Kansas was already at war. When Kansas became a state, people rushed west to claim government-granted land. Many Americans came from as far away as Main and Virginia, while others were from just over the border in Missouri. Free land was what everyone wanted. The problem was many men and women from Missouri wanted their laws indoctrinated, and the easterners didn't. In other words, the Missourians wanted a slave state where they could make bigger plantations to grow hemp and cotton—the two major crops at the time. This agricultural wealth made the south rich and provided much of the food and cloth for the north.

Then came the Industrial Revolution, and the north became wealthy and powerful. All this time, the battle went on between the Jayhawkers and the Bushwhackers, or the pro-slavery population. Violent conflicts cursed the border towns for six years before the Civil War and even continued after. The Lawrence town massacre was a result.

The men who rode with Quantrill's Raiders were war-hardened soldiers. Frank James and the Younger brothers were a few. Bloody Bill Anderson led another band of Raiders with whom rode Jesse James. Despite Frank already in the ranks, William Quantrill found Jesse too young. Something Bloody Bill disagreed with, so he took him on at a mere sixteen. Jesse was already knee-deep in the Missourian Cause, even when young.

A few soldiers were selected for their specific talents. Among them was John Noland. He was a slave on loan by his owner, Francis Asbury Noland. He lent him to Quantrill's Raiders due to his skills in tracking and marksmanship. The captain only trusted John as his scout. Other names became forgotten with time. As always, the victors bore the honor to write history.

Of course, Jesse and Frank James went on to make America's first train robbery. The Younger brothers joined forces, and gangs were formed and merged. Others escaped, mostly south for Texas. A sympathizer with the South but not the fanatics found on the border with Missouri and Kansas.

CHAPTER 1

CAPTAIN QUANTRILL

HORSES' HOOVES CLOPPED OUT OF THE DARKNESS AS Captain William Quantrill appeared in the clearing at the head of a column of two hundred marauders. The setting moon cast a silver glow on the soldiers' faces. Beside him rode John Noland, a Black slave. He was the captain's personal scout and considered irreplaceable. He could track a fish across a river without anyone seeing him.

Behind Quantrill's scout rode a soldier with long black hair and a four-year-old beard. He rode with a Sharps rifle cradled in his arms and hollow eyes; his face was emotionless. He had seen his share of violence and then some. Quantrill's men knew they fought for a lost cause. With nothing more to lose, vengeance was the prime motivator.

The captain's men possessed some of the Confederacy's limited supply of Henry repeater rifles. Quantrill and his soldiers were on the front lines of the struggle in Kansas and Missouri, so they received the best equipment the Southern Army had.

When they pulled the regiment to a halt, Captain Quantrill looked from John to Jedediah Coal. They instinctively knew they would be going on a dangerous mission. Then again, nowhere was safe south of the Mason Dixon. There were no missions that weren't rife with danger. As victory slipped farther away from Southern Army, Quantrill's orders were more desperate. The "cause" no longer seemed to be of importance. All that was left was the deep desire for retribution on the obvious winners before the arrival of the end.

Many of his men wore bloody bandages on their heads, arms, and legs. If they were only winged and not put out of commission, they fought on for the "cause." They pushed their pain aside and let their political fervor give them strength to attack another unbeatable position.

Quantrill seemed obsessed.

The captain nudged his horse close to John and Jed's and said, "We know down the road at the other end of the first open field is half a Yankee regiment. They camped there last night," Captain Quantrill whispered. "But we can't get at them unless we destroy the two howitzers sitting on the hill. There's no way we can sneak a couple of men close enough to blow them up. So, I want you two to make sure when we ride into the valley, we aren't riding into the valley of death. I don't expect to see a single cannon fired. I'll give you two an hour to get into position. That's when we'll make our charge. Is that clear?"

Like two mutes, the men only nodded. Their faces were chiseled in stone. They knew what was expected of them and would give their lives if necessary.

The captain stopped for a moment as he stared hard at Noland and Coal, looking for some sign of weakness.

The captain was a keen observer of men. Sometimes, he knew exactly what his men were thinking.

"Don't let me down, John," Captain Quantrill said. He was as serious as death. "Don't let your fellow Raiders down, men. We're counting on you."

When he turned his gaze to Jed, the young man nearly cringed. William Quantrill had an aurora about him, as if some energy field surrounded him. It made Jed edgy. As the war went on, the captain seemed to become more empowered. It was as though he was on a mission from God. It was the last thing one would expect of an Ohio schoolteacher.

As the column of men dismounted and chewed on dry biscuits and drank water, Jed and John advanced. They tied their horses a safe distance away but close enough to get to them quickly. On foot, they made sure to stay off the trail but always keep it in sight. If the Yankees moved unexpectedly, they would have time to retreat and warn the company of an attack.

They could easily monitor the enemy as they raced through the woods. The Blue Coats were preparing to get under way for the day. Some of the cooks were still cleaning up after breakfast. Other men were saddling their horses. Half a regiment of Union soldiers were right in front of Jed and John. They looked to the right, where two howitzers sat on a hill. A pair of men were driving two teams of workhorses up the steep grade. They intended to back the cannons down and into formation.

The Yankees had no idea Quantrill's Raiders were a mile down the road. John looked at his watch and nudged Jed, giving him the signal to begin. They covered themselves in leafy branches until they looked like walking bushes. They stopped under a tall tree, out of sight of the Yankees. Strapping his rifle over his shoulder, Jed pulled himself up onto the lowest limb and scrambled up the branches like a raccoon. John followed at a slower, more deliberate pace.; He was fifteen years Jed's elder.

Jed sat high in the bow as he lodged himself between tree branches and the trunk. He used his knife to clean the branch in front of him and then rested his Sharps rifle steady. He closed his eyes for a few seconds and focused on calming his breathing and clearing his mind. He detached himself from his actions to block all moral code embedded deep in his soul. He knew if he didn't do a good job, he would be in deep shit. No matter which way he turned, he faced spiritual darkness.

Coal recalled the night when the captain ordered he and John to shoot the Yankees who were robbing the bodies of dead Confederates. They scurried over the corpses like rats, checking one and then another for any valuables. Even after they began shooting, the thieves still tried to elude the bullets and rob the dead. Many died, but others replaced them. Their disregard for life was due to their greed.

Jed knew if he didn't stop the cannon fire, the captain would cut his nuts off and feed them to the squirrels. If the Yankees overran them, they would be dead men, their bodies battered by cannon fire. The only way to survive was to do the best he could. That meant men would die because Jed didn't miss. He moved his scope from one face to another until he recognized his targets. They were four soldiers at each cannon. The howitzers stood side by side.

Jed pulled a long bullet from his jacket. His pockets bulged with 45-75 cartridges, loaded with 405-grain bullets. Yankees called this rifle Beecher's Bible. They believed a single Sharps rifle was worth more than a hundred Southern Bibles.

The bullets Jed used normally were used to kill buffalo. So, they would work today. Two Union soldiers drove the workhorses forward as they slapped their reins across their backs and up the steep grade. The horses snorted and groaned in protest. If they arrived at the top, it would up the ante to ten men Jed had to shoot.

John's spyglass was glued to his eye as he picked out the first target. He whispered into Jed's ear, but he shook his head. He instead took a bead on the man driving the workhorses to the cannon. Jed figured he could get off ten to twelve rounds in a minute.

He pulled the trigger and the gun bucked. The over-sized bullet roared out of the barrel, followed by a flame and a puff of smoke. The lead horse fell, rearing backward, rolling over the second horse and the soldiers driving them.

Jed moved his glass to the cannon and saw two men with spyglasses. They were scouring the hills for the shooter. Jed was so deep in the trees the enemy saw neither the powder flash nor the smoke. It was the perfect cover.

Next, he shot the two sergeants in charge of the howitzers—the men with the spy glasses. The fourth shot put a gaping hole in another soldier's chest. The bullet passed through him and carried on, slamming into a second soldier. It catapulted him back ten feet. Automatically switching off his emotions, Jed surgically eliminated each of the enemy soldiers. His actions were thoughtless. He kept the mission as impersonal as possible.

John tapped his shoulder twice to let him know it was time to go. Things in the Yankee camp were chaotic.

Most of the men hid behind whatever they could find. The sound of heavy-caliber gunshots echoed across the small valley. Suddenly Captain Quantrill and his men burst from the tree line and rode hard toward the enemy. Some were brothers or cousins, but now they wished them dead. The marauders screamed their battle cries as they charged.

Jed and John looked at each other, gathered their things and shimmied down the tree. They led their horses deep into the woods for the whole day. Making sure their silhouettes weren't seen on the horizon. As soon as it was dark, they mounted up and rode south. They pushed their horses hard, not knowing how long it would be before Captain Quantrill discovered they were missing.

They stopped for a moment, and Jed asked, "Don't ya think we could talk the captain into letting us just go home? He knows we've done lost. It's General Lee who is keeping us fighting when we all know we can't win."

"You might as well read the Bible to a buffalo," John replied. "The captain never changes his plans, and he don't give a damn about our lives. All he can see is revenge for the loss to come."

Initially, they hoped the marauders would suspect the sniper team was shot or captured. Even with Quantrill catching the Union army unawares, they knew they couldn't kill them all. They were five hundred well-armed men. They had an endless supply of bullets, something the South had less of every.

They rode through the night without stopping. When morning came, they snuck up on a farmhouse. Laundry hung in a backyard. It was wet, but it would do. The deserters grabbed shirts, pants, and socks and ran for the corral. They took two of their horses and left them theirs. Neither man had ever stolen a thing before, but there was a first time for everything when it came to Civil War.

Like most situations in their lives, the deserters had little choice. They had to get rid of their uniforms and remain unseen. They didn't want to get shot as spies either. They walked on the edge of a knife. The slightest slip, and they would die.

Before long, they knew the United States Marshals, the Union army and their own Missourians would be after them. If they wanted to survive, they had no choice but to run.

CHAPTER 2

JEDIDIAH COAL

THE SILHOUETTES OF TWO RIDERS RAN ACROSS THE ROCKY horizon, tinted gray by the rising moon. Long shadows chased their images as they raced over the distance. The brown cloud of dust following them disappeared as the light waned, and the night kidnapped the day for another twelve hours.

Jed Coal and John Noland knew they would be shot if they were caught by Quantrill's men. Nobody ran off from the captain without expecting a bullet in the back as they fled. Even with the war nearly over, the tension continued to rise in Missouri and Kansas. The first sparks of the Civil War started there ten years earlier. They all knew the streets of both states would run red with blood before it was all over. The newspapers called it "Bloody Kansas."

Every day the Civil War crawled closer to the end. The South was running out of supplies, and things looked grim. Noland and Coal knew they might not have another chance if they didn't run now. Quantrill was on the black-list of the Confederate army after the massacre at Lawrence. If he committed one more atrocity, all hell was going to break loose. They believed it was a matter of weeks before the bands of Raiders disbanded anyway.

Noland overheard Jesse talking to Frank James about robbing banks and trains. Bill Anderson already broke off with his own regiment but died in a bloody battle with Union soldiers. Only Captain Quantrill and George Todd were left. Soon the Union army would deal with anybody still under the command of Captain William Clarke Quantrill just as severely. For those still supporting what remained of the South, unknown evil lurked.

It wasn't like they were in a regular Rebel fighting unit. They were marked as Quantrill's men, perhaps for life. Their only chance was to desert and run. The Raiders were on a path of revenge, and nothing any longer mattered.

Jed hadn't all that much notion of exactly why the war started. He knew it had to do with taxes and the freedom of the states to keep slave labor. Beyond that, he'd hardly had the time to think once they ushered him into the ranks of Quantrill's Raiders. From day one, he ambushed the enemy while on patrol. They were specialists in guerrilla warfare. They brought a new type of battle to the northern forces. Although the morality of the captain's actions was questionable, their superiors often turned a blind eye. It was war.

Both men knew if they were caught, they would face a firing squad. They were hardened to war and knew little else. John was still the best tracker Quintrell ever had and Jed the best shot. The captain wasn't going to be happy when he discovered they both deserted. John was enslaved and still had an owner, which mattered little to Jed.

From the first day Jed joined Quantrill's Raiders, he and John sneaked across enemy lines. The old tracker and scout would find the enemy, and the young Confederate marksman would shoot and kill whoever he pointed out. It was the one thing that always amazed John Noland. Jedediah never missed—even riding flat out from the back of a horse. He was the best shot the Black man ever saw.

Because of their close friendship, John proposed they escape and save themselves from what was to come. The captain had lost all reason and sought revenge against the Kansas Yankees. Of course, the alliances of both Kansas and Missouri were always in question. Captain Quantrill intended to force those in Kansas to change sides if necessary.

While Jed rode in the regiment, he learned military tactics such as disguises, coordinated and synchronized attacks, and planned dispersal after each attack using preplanned routes. They also kept things like relay horses and backup food hidden in locations along their escape routes.

Missouri Bushwhackers favored a particular piece of clothing called the guerrilla shirt. It was a variation of a hunter's coat from the Great Plains. It was a pullover, open deeply down the front. They had four large pockets, two in the breast and two on the sides. The pockets were large enough to hold loads of cartridges and spare pre-loaded revolvers. Some of the Raiders carried as many as six pistols. They all carried Bowie knives. Some even wielded Indian tomahawks.

There wasn't a member of the Raiders who had not seen what the war did to the captain. There was no longer any logic in his actions, just revenge now that the war's outcome seemed inevitable. Neither Jed nor John wanted to go down with him.

The Raiders were tagged Bushwhackers because of their guerrillas tactics. Quantrill's lawless gang included the infamous James brothers, Jesse and Frank. While Jed rode in the regiment, he learned everything his fellow soldiers knew.

Jed's long dark hair and beard fluttered as they fled, and his sharp green eyes searched the path ahead. John was the captain's scout for many years. He was a Black man who knew nothing but bad would come from the crimes the captain committed. In most parts, a Black man on the wrong side of White folks was dangerous. Both men found themselves between a cliff and a river. They were going to have to climb out of their hole or swim the rapids with the rest. They knew it was a matter of time. They doubted there would be another opportunity.

The first year Jed rode with Quantrill's Raiders, he became hardened by the war; it was that or die. The Civil War was a nightmare for all those who survived. The aftermath brought only misery. After the war ended, many had nowhere to go. Jed had yet to return home because all that was left was a burned-out shell of his family's farm in a small town in Louisiana.

Born a Southerner, Jed fought in the war from the day it started. He believed if he stayed with the captain, he would perish before it ended. Coal had prayed for a truce or victory, but knew a successful end was not in store for the South.

Unlike many of the men with whom he rode, Jed escaped the war without a scar. The only trace of his participation was in his eyes. At times, he had a hard time focusing on things far away. Other than that, the only difference was the legality of his actions. With the war nearly over, the Raiders found themselves on the wrong side of victory and the law. Of course, the captain held little regard for Yankee law.

As the war went on, Jed found there was the way things should be, and there was the way things were. One had little to do with the other. No matter how many raids they made, nothing was going to change.

In recent months, he saw how recklessly they fought and randomly targets were selected. He saw they were attacking those who had what the Raiders needed in food and ammunition. Things often didn't stop there either. Atrocities were committed, too—not by Jed or John, but by men like Bloody Bill Anderson's Marauders and Todd's Guerrillas.

When Jed joined the Confederate army, he knew what side he was on. Now, he recognized his government's leaders made a mistake. They lost the war, and nobody could do anything about it. It was time to try to find peace.

There was on big problem. After riding with Quantrill's Raiders, his name would soon be on the lists in every US Marshal's office across the South. Instead of meeting his fate in Kansas or Missouri, he decided to take a chance and run for the Territories and beyond?

Of course, the Indian Territories of Oklahoma were still dangerous to cross. They would have to make their way down the Chisholm Trail. Maybe they could latch on with a wagon train or a bunch of cowboys returning from a cattle drive. Where there were numbers, there was safety, a lesson he learned riding with Quintrell.

They pulled up on the top of a hill to see if soldiers followed. Jed's piercing green eyes caught the last light of the day, and his black hair and beard blew in the afternoon breeze. He pulled off his straw hat and wiped his brow with the sleeve of his checkered shirt. Both men discarded their Raider's shirts and hats as soon as they broke ranks with the captain. They wore clothing they robbed from a backyard clothesline.

Quantrill's Raiders also got the spoils of war. With no place to spend money during the conflict, both sniper and scout saved what they confiscated from dead bodies. Most of the currency was Yankee, which was still valuable after the war. The cash and coinage of the Confederacy was worthless.

They used what they learned and disguised themselves. They even changed their horses and saddles, so they bore no Confederate brands. In their time with the Raiders, they learned how to ambush and escape nearly every situation a man could imagine. They did it day in and out. They applied those same skills in flight.

Their first objective was to bypass Fort Worth and head for San Angelo, Texas, where John said he had a family. Quantrill's Raiders wintered in Texas near Cedar Mills and, while there, helped with the Texans' cause. Jed knew they would be a hell of a lot safer there than on the border with Kansas and Missouri. The faster they got away, the safer they would be.

They stopped for a rest at a water hole along the way. Jed always kept his Sharps rifle within reach, lifesaving habits acquired over years at war were engrained in his behavior. Especially when he suspected the captain would send men after them.

Francis Asbury Noland loaned John to the Raiders because of his keen hunting and tracking skills. However, no one treated him like a slave in the captain's ranks. He was respected as any other man in the unit. Only the captain was more revered.

Although John remained enslaved and with no say of his own, the captain saw he received one of the seventeen hundred Henry rifles the Confederate states acquired for its sniper teams. It was a sixteen-shot, .44 caliber rimfire breech-loading, lever-action rifle—the weapon of choice through the Civil War. Jed was given a confiscated rifle from a Union sniper. It was a .52 caliber Sharps single-shot long rifle with a telescopic scope.

When they finally arrived in Oklahoma, Jed saw a newspaper while shopping for supplies. They wanted to know if word was out about two deserters, one Black and the other White. They would be easy enough to spot, especially in the South. So, John hid in an alley while Jed gathered supplies and information.

With a canvas sack full of salted pork, beans, and coffee, Jed went around to the alley where John was waiting. The sniper also shaved off several years of beard and trimmed his hair. He looked like another person when he stepped into the shadows of the alley.

"Lord have mercy!" John declared. "You look like a different fella with a haircut. It does nothin' but good for your looks." Of course, he laughed uproariously.

The lack of beard was easily visible by the contrast of dark sun-tanned skin above white cheeks and chin.

"You bought a new hat and all," John declared.

"I just read the newspaper," Jed declared. "The war's over. General Robert E. Lee surrendered."

"It was about time," John said. "That will only increase the confusion."

A flat black leather hat sat over his neatly trimmed hair. You could even see his ears. Jed had hardly shaved since signing on. Hell, there was rarely the opportunity other than on those short stints in Texas where the weather was mild. San Angelo was known for hot, one-hundred-degree summers and cool winters, but it rarely snowed.

"We ain't free yet," John said as he eyed the bright, sunlit street from the shadows of the alley. "We better be careful until we get to central Texas. I figure the farther south, the better. Most folks there didn't take a stand one way or another as far as the war goes. In West Texas, they say folks hardly paid any mind to it at all."

"Look, I got me a pair of new boots too," Jed said and almost smiled.

John was surprised. He had never seen Jed crack even a slight smile during their entire time together. He looked like he was almost there, but nothing happened. John never saw a man more serious in his entire life.

"I'm surprised you could find a size twelve boot." John cackled as he looked at his young accomplice. "Now that you've disguised yourself; what are we gonna do about me?"

They believed John best stay hidden until they were in Texas. So, they often rode at night. They mounted up and headed south. Texas was still a southern state and aligned with the Confederacy. They believed they would be safe in the far south, though. Eastern Texas saw little of the war, and there was even less law.

Jed wasn't a young man anymore; he felt old. Over the years, he learned most of what John and the captain had to teach. Most of what he learned from the captain was about killing other men and getting away. What he learned from John was about living. He was like a sponge when it came to learning, though. He'd always been that way.

Jed grew up toiling on the family farm. The Coals owned a few acres of land that were surrounded by large plantations. The Coal family never enslaved a person, so

Jed considered the slavery issue was for rich folks. Many people in Missouri claimed it was all about states' rights. He still understood little when it came to politics, but he did know about the battle between Kansas and Missouri for the last ten years. From what he gathered, there was more to it than the right to enslave people. Most of that neither he nor John would ever understand.

Jed was a well-read man, something special for a soldier. John couldn't read or write. In the south, education was an issue with slaves. The plantation owners found the less education slaves had, the less resistance they seemed to put up. The Coal children had an educated mother, though. She taught them from as early as Jed could remember.

Since Jed grew up dirt poor, he hardly saw any difference between himself and John. They worked together as a sniper team for the last four years. They had each other's back in all types of dangerous situations. Men who experience such things together find color was only skin deep. Now, Jed could track as good as John—almost.

They were elite soldiers even if they did fight for the losing side. For doing what Jed thought was right; he found himself in a desperate situation. John never had a say in the matter but he, too, suffered the consequences.

CHAPTER 3

JODI GOODNIGHT

Jodi PUSHED HERSELF DEEP INTO THE SHADOWS AS SHE waited in the alley at the edge of the building. This wasn't the first time a drunken fool grabbed her ass, and it probably wouldn't be the last. If men in the west saw a pretty girl in a saloon having a drink, they immediately got the wrong idea. Torches burned bright all along the street in Waco, Texas, casting flickering shadows on the buildings. The light didn't reach the dark alley, where a wildcat patiently waited in the dark. She had her Navy Colt revolver in her fist. The only place her anger showed was in the white-knuckles that gripped the six-gun's handle.

After a time, light spilled out onto the street as someone pushed the saloon doors open. Three drunken men staggered out into the night. They each had a bottle of spirits in one hand and a pistol in the other. They appeared to be just a few cowboys blowing off steam—but there were limits to what Jodi permitted in her presence. Poor manners and sass weren't on that list and grabbing at her ass was on the top of what not to do.

Without a pistol and a knife, she looked like a typical country girl. Dressed as she was, her shapely figure hidden, it was easy to mistake her for a boy. She wore old denim britches that shrank too much with time. A cotton checked shirt and a denim jacket hid her shapely breasts—almost. Her shiny hair was black and long and highlighted her sun-tanned face from years in the Texas sun. When she turned those fiery blue eyes on a man, she could pin him to a wall and make his cojones drop to the ground.

The man who grabbed her in the Walnut Saloon walked into the night as lightning bugs flashed in the dark alley. He and his friends reeked of stale whiskey and days of sweat.

"Ya lookin' for me, sweetie?" Jodi said with a flirtatious smile. She hid her revolver behind her back as she flashed her eyes and winked.

The drunken ruffian swung toward the soft voice and grinned a mouth full of yellow teeth.

"Here I am. Can't ya see me, darlin'?" he said. "Come on over here. Let me show ya somethin'."

He staggered toward her with a wicked grin. As slick as spit, Jodi hit him across the face with the barrel of her revolver. The sharp gunsight sliced a cut from the top of his cheek to his chin. It lay open like a filet. Jodi was no fool, though. She knew, as a woman, she had to be twice as devious, and three times as mean to survive alone. It was that or go and work in a pleasure palace, and, for her, that was not what she called survival. She would die before she gave up and sought employment as a whore.

The Civil War had just ended. Chaos and confusion ran rampant across the South, including the state of Texas. The war was hell, but this was hell, too. Men outnumbered single women three hundred to one if you didn't count the prostitutes. Tens of thousands of directionless men wandered south once the war was lost.

Only the married women, those living on ranches, or the very rich, who had guards to protect them, survived in the environment: Texas was not a safe place after the war, evidence was all around.

The two friends of the fallen man began to protest, but Jodi's eyes followed her gun barrel toward the voices and said, "I don't tolerate bad manners in a man. That'll teach y'all not to treat women poorly."

One of his drunken friends asked, "Are you all right, Sheriff?" Blood pooled under his face as he lay unconscious on the wooden porch.

One of the men kneeled and checked the sheriff's pulse and found his heart was still thumping. After a few minutes, he began to come around. He was dizzy, confused and still dead drunk. He didn't notice the cut on his face until he wiped his nose, and his hand came away bloody. His face turned the color of a cherry. He was about to blow a gasket.

When he got up and saw his reflection in a glass window, he howled like a wounded dog. It gave his friends such a fright they instantly sobered up.

"Where the hell is that bitch?" Sheriff Charles Conan yelled. "Assaulting an officer with intent to murder is a hanging offense."

"I don't think she was planning to murder nobody, Charles," his sheriff's friend replied. "I do believe she thought you were just another cowboy. You ain't wearing your badge and ya did grab her ass."

Sheriff Conan was young and looked more like a cowpoke than a sheriff. That's what he was before he was a soldier. He wasn't the type of man to let a woman best him, though. It was intolerable, especially with a couple of his friends looking on during his first night on the job. He had too much pride for that.

"Damn, she sure did take a slice out of ya," George Mills said. He was so drunk he had difficulty not snickering and making the sheriff angrier.

As soon as Jodi realized she had assaulted the new town sheriff, she knew not to stick around. The ranch was pretty much gone, and everything stolen. She had little to lose but her freedom and maybe even her life. In Waco, Texas, they did hang the odd woman, especially now that the war had ended.

She had tied her horse at the end of the alley. Nobody could see her when she ran for her mare and jumped into the saddle. She shot out of town like her hair was on fire. She pushed her horse for all it was worth for the first miles. She knew enough about horses to back off, so she didn't bake her.

Jodi Goodnight wasn't afraid of any man, but she knew they would make an example of her if they chased her down.

It was too embarrassing for the upstart who replaced the old Confederate sheriff. She made a fool of the Yankee in front of his friends, a thing that never stayed quiet. There was always some blabbermouth who would spill the beans, and the new town hero would have his image tarnished by a woman.

Lately, Jodi had so much bad luck she couldn't remember how good luck felt. She rode through the night, being careful to avoid gopher holes and slippery trails. It rained earlier that day, and the trails were still partially muddy.

When it was nearly light, she decided to find a gully, make a small fire and prepare something to eat and heat some coffee. A person on the run had to keep up their strength. As she carefully selected her way across the countryside, she knew as soon as the sun rose, she would be visible. Jodi believed it would be safest if she hid by day and rode by night. She collected only the driest wood for her small fire to reduce the smoke.

She hobbled her mare and let her graze on the sparse grass in the gorge. At least their silhouettes won't show on the horizon as the sun began to rise. Before she knew it, the hot summer rays bore down on her. She made her fire and cooked some frying pan biscuits and beans. When it started to sprinkle, she huddled under a ledge in the gully wall as she ate her hot meal. Soon the rain drowned the fire. As she sat, she watched a little puddle of water turn into a stream. As the rain increased, the gully became a small river.

Jodi and her mare, Sandy, made it to high ground. As soon as they reached the top of the gorge and looked across the landscape, she saw the clouds and mist were thick. It may be uncomfortable riding in the rain, but she had to do the best she could with what little she had. Soon the rain was coming down in a downpour.

Bolts of lightning began to drop from the skies and punish the earth. A tree nearby where they walked lay lightning racked. So, Jodi stepped down from her horse to create a lower profile and steered away from the trees. Standing out in a lightning storm was dangerous, but it was more hazardous under a big tree.

On several occasions, she had seen trees hit by lightning, and it fried all the cattle standing below. The lightning shot straight through the tree, into the roots, and up and into the unsuspecting livestock. She imagined this happening to her and shuddered.

Everywhere she looked, danger seemed to lurk. She was aware of the Comanche that populated these lands too. She suddenly realized a woman entirely on her own in the vast Texas wilderness had enemies on all fronts.

CHAPTER 4

JOHN NOLAND

OUT OF HABIT, THE BLACK SCOUT ALWAYS CIRCLED BACK around two or three times a day to ensure nobody followed the deserters. The former slave could track a snake across a river and never lose its trail. He was surprised when he came across the signs of a single horse. He and Jed took an exceptionally rugged path to increase the odds of going undetected. He hadn't expected to find anybody following them that wasn't Comanche. He simply did as they always did in enemy territory—be as careful as possible.

Since they were on the run for desertion from the Missouri Raiders and wanted by the Yankees for riding with Quantrill and Bloody Bill Anderson, they had to be twice as careful. In a newspaper along the trail, Jed read William Quantrill was in route to Ohio when he was shot and killed in an ambush by Union soldiers in Lexington, Kentucky. He died only a month after the end of the war. Jed saw the posted article weeks after his death.

Bloody Bill Anderson fell out with Quantrill and

formed his own Rebel Raiders a couple of years before the war ended and took the young Jesse James to ride with him. Soon, he was considered more dangerous than Quantrill. He died in a desperate gun battle, however, on October 26, 1864.

When Quantrill walked away, some men went home and others followed Anderson, and Todd's predecessors on their crusade for revenge. Among those were Frank and Jesse James, along with James, John, and Thomas Younger. They all were men Jed and John rode with during much of the war. Cole Younger was an officer in the regular Confederate army.

The scout rode back out front, where Jed was carefully picking a challenging trail to follow. He always kept his eyes on the Texas horizon, looking for danger. The scout knew it was dangerous riding during the day, but they were good at traveling alone when they weren't with the captain. John couldn't figure out why somebody was out there on their own. He could only believe the tracks he saw were following them.

The ancient trail they took was hardly a trail at all, and every chance they got, they concealed their flight from anyone who might give chase. Noland technically was still a slave, though his owner was from Missouri. He knew it would be some time before the folks on the border with Kansas would recognize the freedom of enslaved people.

After the war ended, the conflicts continued on the border. They started six years before the Civil War began, so it stood to reason it would continue years after. There was so much hate in that part of America; one atrocity or massacre after another took place. Somebody was always looking to get even for a crime committed by the other side.

Jed didn't believe change would come soon, and John knew so little about politics he hardly understood what it was to be a free man. They both knew the folks in the South would take longer to become accustomed to the rules of the North. Hell, Jed was just glad he was still alive, and the war was over. He never doubted for a moment the Yankee Army would ever forget who the men were who rode with Quantrill's Raiders, including a slave like John Noland. Everyone who fled would be hunted down and executed.

Men like Jesse James participated in the vilest fighting and became so hardened, there was no hope of turning straight. Frank seemed to come from a different mold than his younger brother. Jesse was just sixteen when he signed on with the Confederacy and submerged himself in Missouri politics against the Kansas Jayhawkers. Captain Quantrill never allowed him to join the Raiders because he was too young. Jesse was the first to sign up when Bloody Bill Anderson split off. When the war ended, the James brothers, and others like them, no longer were suitable for anything other than armed conflict.

Jed heard after the war, the Yankees captured Jesse's sister and mother. They destroyed their home. In Jed's eyes, Jesse was forced into the world of violence in which he lived. Frank just followed on to keep an eye on his younger brother. Only Jesse's extreme prejudice set him apart and made him a natural leader, despite the fact Frank was six years older.

When Noland reported to Jed what he found, they both began to look for the best place to set up an ambush. It was what they did for the last four years as soldiers in Quantrill's Raiders. Both men had the patience of a panther as they waited for their prey to round the bend. They chose a high hill with a clear field of fire and a good view down the trail from where they came. An hour passed and then two, as they sat motionless, Noland with a spyglass glued to his eye and Jed looking through the scope of his long rifle.

As they patiently waited, they first saw a small cloud of dust. Yesterday's rain dried under the blistering sun, and the dirt turned to a fine powder and billowed behind the horse.

The scout elbowed Jed as both turned their eyes on the rider wearily walking up the sinuous trail. John Noland was the spotter and let Jed know when the target was in range. Then Jed would take careful aim and fire a single shot. Corporal Coal never needed more than one bullet per target.

Hell, he'd even shot two men with one bullet a couple of times. They were riding double at the time. The heavy-caliber Sharps rifle round went right through the first Yankee and into the heart of the second. He had shot men from hundreds of yards away during the Civil War. All snipers were required to keep a tally of the men they killed. Jed never talked about those numbers. Only the captain and John knew the truth.

Coal liked to keep his missions as impersonal as possible and tried to kill each man quickly. He prided himself in turning their lights out so fast they never knew what hit them.

Noland never questioned their orders. In the South, slaves weren't allowed an opinion. Quantrill trusted old John more than the corporal. He always gave Noland the targets and locations. Then, the scout would lead Jed to who he was supposed to shoot.

As their pursuer came into view, Jed pulled back the hammer on his long rifle. The only noise apart from crickets was the click of the gun. He focused on his target and took a bead as he placed his finger beside the trigger guard.

~

THE MARE LED Jodi along a barely visible trail faithfully and without complaint. They picked their way down what she suspected to be an old unused Indian path. The mare suddenly shook her head and squealed.

Jodi stopped dead in her tracks. She held her breath as she squatted and listened. Her eyes studied the horizon, looking for what spooked her horse. Traveling off the beaten path was dangerous but not as hazardous as what awaited her back in Waco.

She dared not ride her horse because they still kicked up a small cloud of dust even with them ambling. Her pistol was in her hand. The chamber engaged as she thumbed back the hammer. It sounded ten times louder than she anticipated. The wind whistled in the grass, but she couldn't hear anything else. Her horse continued to pull on the reins and shift her hooves.

Jodi dropped the reins and pulled her bandana off, wiping her neck dry and the sweat out of her eyes. All the time, her gaze followed the barrel of her Colt revolver. The fiery disk above bore down as the heat baked everything for as far as she could see.

When the crickets went quiet, Jodi knew eyes were upon her. A chill when up her spine at the thought of a band of Comanche catching her. She thought back on an article about White women captured by the natives. The newspaper said it was preferable to die by one's own bullet than to succumb to the hostiles and torture.

Well, Jody sure as hell didn't plan to kill herself. But if

Comanche were out there waiting, she intended to give them a lesson in manners they wouldn't soon forget, even if she died in the process. The woman was so strong-willed and hardheaded, she would be hobbled by neither man nor woman.

She saw the impact of the bullet before she heard the report. It slammed into a giant cactus to her left. When the second bullet exploded a small tree to her right, she dived for a small outcrop of rocks. After the first shot, Sandy ran for the hills.

~

"YOU MISSED," John said in shock. Another shot rang out, and he said, "You missed again. What the hell's wrong with you?"

All the time, the scout had the spyglass glued to his eye. He saw one round slam into a cactus, and the other blew a mesquite tree to smithereens. Jed continued to look down the scope. He saw the rider jump for the rocks right before the horse ran off.

"She must be hiding behind that crop of stones," Jed said as he looked at John. "I don't shoot women. Even Captain Quantrill was against killing women and children, and that was in the war. Unfortunately, I can't say the same about Bloody Bill Anderson."

Noland's eyes spread wide in surprise. He never imagined a woman so foolish as to ride such country unescorted.

"There must be more folks with her," John said. "Townsfolk don't think much of White women traipsing around the country all alone. I thought you'd lost your touch for a minute there, what with you missin' twice and all."

Jed stared at the Army scout with sparkling eyes and said, "I never miss, John. You know that."

"Whatcha wanna do?" the Black man asked. "We can't leave her out there on her own, especially now that there's been gunfire. The Comanche could have heard us. We've gotta move and fast."

"We might be mean sons-of-bitches, but we're still southern gentlemen," Jed replied stone-faced. "I reckon I might remember some manners."

"If she rides along with you and me, she may well end up being wanted by the Army like us," John said.

"Well, we can always leave her out there," Jed replied. "We've probably already got enough trouble trailing us as it is."

They fell silent for a spell as they watched the crop of rocks in the distance. Whoever it was, they were pinned down at least until dark. But they worried. The sound of their gunshots could have carried for miles.

Despite being former Rebel soldiers, John and Jed no longer were fervent supporters. They had both seen enough killing and bloodshed and wanted to try to change their lives. Neither of them chose to join Quantrill's Raiders; the captain forced them into the regiment. It will be up to the Yankee Army and the Missouri Raiders to decide if they will be allowed to live or not.

CHAPTER 5

UNWANTED COMPANY

"Whatcha think we should do, John?" Jed whispered. "We can't wait out here all day. If the Raiders did send men to track us down, they're going to find the girl first. Do you think they'll go hard on her?"

"What do you care?" Noland asked in a hushed voice. "You don't know her. I think we'd best just be on our way. It's clear she's not following us. She was just wandering around out here like some damned fool."

As they waited, everything seemed too quiet. The safety they felt a while before vanished like a buffalo's breath on a cold morning. Neither man knew what to expect. Of course, they weren't sure anyone would follow them all the way to Texas. Then again, it would take the Union army a while to track them this far south. Even if Missourians weren't chasing them, they knew there would be wanted posters out for both of them soon, if not already.

Nobody who rode with Quantrill would be spared. Neither man had any choice in what they did or what company they rode with. They followed orders or they would have been shot you on the spot. Quantrill never hesitated to shoot men who cowered in combat. They knew there would be repercussions and no mercy.

Even if Noland was a free man, he doubted the Yankees would take his word that he was just following his owner's orders, scouting for the Raiders. Everyone who rode with Quantrill will have a price on his head. Especially now, as the war had just ended and the wounds of many were still fresh in everyone's mind.

Noland collapsed his spyglass and turned to where they hobbled the horses. Jed grumbled and spat into the dirt. Clearly, he was undecided what to do. He knew the safest thing would be to leave the woman out there, whoever she was. If the Missourians or Yankees were following them, it won't go good for her, though. They might even think she was aiding their flight. Why else would a woman be wandering out here all on her own? He didn't doubt if the Yankees thought she was in cahoots with the Raiders, they would treat her poorly. He saw a lot of abuse during the war. The spoils go to the victors—just like the winners would write the history.

"Don't ya think it's high time we did something good for a change?" Jed asked with raised eyebrows. "What if we have Yankee scouts trailing us? What do you think they'll do to her? She's probably a Southerner."

"Well, make up your mind one way or another. I doubt it be healthy to hang around here too much longer. Even if nobody is on our trail, this is Comanche country. Somebody could have heard those shots."

"My upbringing won't let me leave a woman here to die, no matter what we've become as a result of the war.

Here, take my rifle and keep a good eye on me. I'm going to find out who she is," Jed said. "I hope she don't take a shot at me."

"I doubt she thought kindly of the two shots you took at her." Noland chuckled. "She don't know you meant to miss. Hell, I didn't even know you were shooting wide on purpose."

Jed was a highly experienced sniper, so he knew how to sneak up on people almost as good as an Indian. He'd been sneaking up on Yankees for years. He swung around whoever it was behind the rocks, making sure he made as little noise as possible. Finally, he could see her black hair spill out from under the back of her hat. It sparkled in the sunlight. She was lying on the ground with a big Navy Colt in her fist and had it aimed into the distance. Jed knew Noland would have him in his sights by now, so he carefully moved forward.

The last thing he expected was to be attacked by a horse, and her mare was racing up from behind him. He heard the mare's hooves before she got close, but there was no doubt the horse was gonna run him over. Jed drew and swung the barrels of his Colt Walkers toward the horse and took a bead.

"Don't you dare shoot my horse!" a voice came from behind him.

Jodi whistled, and Sandy stopped her charge and wandered over to her owner. She stood before Jed with a pistol in her fist.

"That horse protects you like a dog," Jed said as he stood up straight. His mouth formed a hard line. Since the woman had the drop on him, he slipped his six-guns into their holsters. He'd never shot a woman yet, and hoped he wouldn't have to.

"My pistol barks and bites, too," the strappy young

woman said. "You'd think with two shots, you should have been able to hit me. You must be the worst shot in Texas."

She was chipping at a chink in Jed's honor. He took most things in stride but not his shooting skills. If it weren't for his dead shot, neither Noland nor he would have survived the war.

"I assure you if I was aiming to kill ya—I'd have shot ya dead," Jed said in a deadpan voice. "Do you know how dangerous it is to travel out here all alone, especially after the war? There be droves of riffraff headin' this way to escape repercussions."

"Is that what you're doin'?" the young woman asked. The sass in her voice stung the corporal.

"I was gonna ask if you wanted to ride with us," Jed said. "I reckon my guilt from the war made me stop and check on ya. My partner didn't think it was a good idea. I'm beginning to think the same."

"Is there somebody else out there?" the cowgirl asked as she turned to glance from where the bullets came. A worried look flashed across her face for just a second.

"Go ahead and smile for Noland." Jed chuckled. "That way, he can see you through the rifle's telescopic sight. We be snipers—at least, we were snipers. Now, I don't rightly know what we are."

Jodi looked from the clean-shaven man and back to where his partner must be. He was supposed to be hiding with a rifle on them both.

"I was a ranch owner, but I made a mistake," she replied. "I don't rightly know what I am either. If you know what's good for ya, you'll go on about your way. I've got the Waco sheriff on my tail. I got the feeling you boys got enough of your own problems."

"Are you any good with that pistol, or is it just for decoration?" Jed asked.

"You wanna find out?" she said, immediately turning mean again.

"Hold on there," Jed said as he held up his hands. "I was offering for you to ride with us, so you don't get caught by Comanche. If it makes ya feel any better, we're most likely getting chased, too. My name is Jed Coal, and my friend out yonder with the rifle pointed at us is John Noland. He was my spotter during the war."

"From your accent, I reckon y'all be from the south. My name's Jodi—Jodi Goodnight—and I don't dabble in politics. No matter which side you pick, you're always mistaken. I never did and never will."

"If you're gonna go with us, stop pointing that damn gun at me before Noland gets the wrong idea and shoots ya dead," Coal said and turned to head back the way he came.

He didn't even wait to see if Jodi was coming or not. He knew it was time to get the hell out of there, and he didn't plan on staying a minute longer. It was up to her if she wanted to come or not. He invited her to ride along, so he'd done his good deed.

"Shit," Jodi spat. Then she whistled again, and her mare came back. She grabbed the reins and followed the soldier. "Hold on there, Mr. Coal. I'm comin'."

Jodi figured she couldn't be any worse off than she currently was. So, she followed the stranger, even though she still wasn't convinced he was telling her the truth. She made sure she was far enough behind him she would have time to pull and fire her pistol if he turned on her. She also was eager to see who was waiting for him or if he was bluffing.

She realized she could be going from the pot to the

frying pan, but she had little choice at this point. She knew all about Comanche from skirmishes at the ranch a couple of years back. With the war on, they got mighty bold in Texas. They thought they could come to her home and take whatever they wanted. She and her pa changed their plans.

Reluctantly, she followed. The stranger was a hard-looking man who could not have been over thirty-five years old. The war aged him. Strangely enough, she saw no scars, unlike most the men she saw return from the debauchery. Somehow, she knew he had gazed into the deeper depths of hell, though. She saw it in his eyes. Those were things he couldn't hide.

When she walked into a small clearing, she saw two horses and a Black man sitting on a rock with a long rifle in his hands. He was puffing on a cheap cheroot.

"Here she is, Noland. This here be Jodi Goodnight," Jed announced.

"Like the Texas rancher?" John asked.

"You didn't tell me you had a slave," Jodi said bitterly. "I told ya I don't dabble in politics, and owning slaves is part of what I don't dabble in."

Both men were serious for a moment, until John burst out laughing. Jed remained as sober as a stone. The Black soldier had to hold his side when he got a stitch.

"We be partners, ma'am," John Noland said between bursts of laughter. "I was a slave, not Jed's though. He ain't the type. My owner is back in Missouri hopefully."

Finally, when he could catch his breath, he added, "Ain't that right, Massa Jedidiah?"

John found this even funnier and rolled with laughter. Jodi was more puzzled than she was before. She wondered if the two weren't crazy, one laughing uproariously and the other as mute as a tree stump.

"We best be gettin' out of here. We've made far too much noise," Jed said.

"I've got a few questions first," Jodi interrupted. Both walked away like they didn't care if she came or not.

As Jed trudged down the trail, he said, "We can talk later. Right now, let's put some distance between us and those gunshots."

CHAPTER 6

SHELTER

THEY WALKED THEIR HORSES OVER ROUGH TERRAIN FOR the rest of the day. They only stopped to water their mounts and take a drink themselves. Even then, nobody spoke a word or explained anything. Jodi was wary and confused. The whole situation seemed strange, so she decided to focus on keeping up.

The men walked at a furious pace and rode their horses less than half the time. The unwitting cowgirl-turned-outlaw rode with the best, but her boots weren't made for walking on rough terrain.

She followed as if she was caught in a rip current and washing out to sea. The rush of water swept her away into the unknown. She didn't know the two men but knew anybody who made it through the Civil War was no daisy, especially anyone who was part of a sniper team.

Even though they traveled fast, both men gathered scraps of wood or dead plants they could later use for a fire. It was immediately apparent they knew exactly what they were doing. Jodi watched them out of the corner of her eye, but it didn't matter. Both men completely ignored her. They appeared to be wholly absorbed in their task.

As they moved south, the Black man always led. Every half hour or so, he would stop and check some track or broken branches. It was almost dark when the scout began to find the best place for them to rest for the night. They trudged up a steep hill on a narrow path until suddenly she found herself in a clearing surrounded by rocks.

From a distance, one could not see a pathway to the top. If anybody followed, they would have to scale the hill on a path wide enough for a single horse to pass. The three at the top would have an invincible position to defend.

Within a half hour, there was a small fire burning in the center of the clearing. A fine trail of smoke rose from the flames and vanished just a few yards over their heads. The smell of coffee and salted pork sizzling over the fire filled the air. As the sun crept toward the end of the world, the sky exploded in a prism of color. Stars began to appear and twinkle on the eastern horizon.

While the men busied themselves, Jodi brushed down and hobbled the horses. She let them nibble at the scarce grass in the clearing. Sandy slid her jaw on some plants and whisked her tail. The men had tin pans filled with pork and beans and fresh biscuits when she finished. It was a long ride, and until today, she had survived on what she could scrape together. It was a luxury to have a warm meal, though. She made her way over to the fire with a pan in hand.

Both Jed and John forked pork and beans into their

mouths and didn't even look up as Goodnight helped herself. An hour and two coffees later, everybody seemed to be relaxed. Jed looked over at Jodi like she was a second thought. Maybe he had forgotten entirely about her. Both men did seem engrossed in their traveling routine. There was no messing around or small talk. Neither of them had spoken since they took a couple of shots at her earlier.

John looked at the woman, trying to figure her out while Jed cleaned his guns. He didn't seem to be interested in her in the slightest. The scout's curiosity got the best of him, though. He couldn't help but wonder how a woman her age could end up on the run. He still hadn't decided if her company was good or bad. She did keep up all afternoon, and they hadn't slowed their escape from unseen enemies.

John thought back on just before Jed took a couple of warning shots at the White woman. He had felt someone was watching them. When the woman showed up, he simply assumed it was her. The feeling stayed with him throughout the day, though.

Captain Quantrill used to say John could smell trouble and kept him close during the entire war. Despite the darkness of their location, he smelled that familiar odor and felt haunting eyes on their every move. That was why he found an extra safe place to spend the night. If there was someone out there, chances were tonight they would find out who it was.

Jed and John were doing the same thing they'd been doing since the beginning of the Civil War. Only now, they didn't have any orders to follow or targets to pursue. Their only targets would be men wanting to kill them or bring them back to Missouri for processing in a

Yankee court. They would be hanged immediately following a guilty verdict.

After supper, the silence continued as the men cleaned and prepared their weapons. Jodi hadn't fired her pistol that day, but she followed suit. The men never cleaned two rifles at the same time. One stood guard over the other during the process. They obviously were preparing for something. For what, Jodi didn't have a clue. Obviously, the men had much more experience than she did at hiding and fleeing.

She studied the Black man and wondered why he was running and from what. If he was a slave, he should be free to do whatever he wanted, even though it would take Missouri some time to accept defeat. Of course, Jodi followed the war. The entire country did. Somehow, though, it seemed harder to envision from Texas.

Jodi spied the Rebel scout from the corner of her eyes. Standing up, Noland was an inch short of Jed's height and his matted hair showed gray around his ears. His face was wrinkled and scarred from the war. His eyes were like dark pools of water, deep and calm.

He sniffed the air as he stood guard with his Henry repeater rifle aimed toward the only trail to their camp-site. Jodi figured a man would have to be half billy goat to climb that steep path at night.

It wasn't a half hour later when John levered a round into his rifle, and Jed looked up from his disassembled revolver. He jumped to his feet and kicked dirt over the fire. Darkness dropped like a curtain around them. Only the moon stared down from above, allowing a little grayish light as white clouds passed between the earth and sky.

Neither man seemed to notice Jodi when she crept forward with her Navy Colt in her fist. Finally, Jed looked back when she scuffed her boot and frowned. He noticed beads of sweat populate her brow. Her eyes were wide but her gun hand seemed steady. So, he turned back to the danger.

Two coyotes called out in the dark. Every time a cloud passed overhead, the darkness deepened. With each passing cloud, Jodie thought she could hear something move in the night. She wasn't sure, though. When John whispered something into Jed's ear, the White soldier nodded.

He slid a long shell into the Sharp's rifle, peered down the scope and waited. At first, Jed couldn't see anything. It was like he was staring into a black hole. Then the cloud passed, and a soft silver light shone from the moon; he could see the outline of the first man scaling the path.

The report of the long gun seemed so loud Jodi nearly jumped out of her skin. It echoed off the rock walls. After came a second report as Jed reloaded the single-shot rifle in a split second and took a bead on at his next target. John lay beside him with his spyglass glued to his eye.

The spotter again whispered to Jed, and this time, Jodi heard what he said: "We got two Comanche down and two more retreating. Do you want to take the shot? You can get a bead on 'em before they get to the bottom."

Jed lay silent as he got the farthest Comanche in his crosshairs. The Indian was running, so he led him a little. He calculated the downward trajectory.

He slowly let out his breath, slipped his finger into the trigger guard and released the safety. The metal click seemed loud, although he knew it wasn't. He peered down the scope at the black silhouette. Only a second remained before a cloud covered the moon. He was ready to shoot. Then he sighed and closed his eyes.

"Maybe today we're gonna let 'em go," Jed whispered.

John gave him the oddest look. It was clear his decision caught the spotter off guard. Jed got up and walked back to his bedroll as he reloaded his Sharps. Then he lay down and went to sleep with his rifle cradled in his arms. Suddenly, he looked exhausted.

Jodi looked back toward the trail and saw John sitting on the ground with his rifle cradled in his arms and his spyglass lying beside him. He continued to stand guard but didn't believe the Comanche would have another go at them. They were looking for something easy to steal while the White men slept. Apparently, they saw it was not such an easy task.

John Noland dressed well for a slave, Jodi thought. She didn't know what to think of him. When Jed huddled under his blanket with his head resting on his saddle, he immediately began to snore. She believed he looked older than he was. They were both strange men.

Jodi felt a bit of a sting from earlier that day. Every young woman alive wanted to get noticed, but she didn't get a glance from John, or Jed. She never was very good at figuring men out, and these two appeared incredibly peculiar.

She momentarily looked back on the life she had and where she found herself now. How did she get here so quickly? Not two years ago, her father was still alive and, despite the war, they were getting along well. They sold many of their beeves to the Confederacy to supply food for their soldiers. Many ranchers never got paid for their cattle. Those that did, got paid in Confederate currency.

As soon as the South surrendered, the southern money wasn't worth a penny. Those who rode out of the storm and survived went under due to a bankrupt government and worthless currency.

Then, the rustling and stealing started. Men who never thought of committing such acts became common criminals once they were no longer soldiers. They wandered south and stole to feed their families.

CHAPTER 7

SOUTHBOUND

IT WAS STILL DARK WHEN JOHN NUDGED JODI'S SHOULDER with the toe of his boot, bringing her out of restless sleep. She dreamed of Comanche climbing the hill in the dark. The first traces of sun showed on the hill to their east and was beginning its slow crawl across the country, shooing away all the silvery shadows with fiery light.

Jodi walked over to the edge and looked down the path, but she saw no dead Comanche as she expected. She peered across the horizon, but she didn't see another living thing.

She looked back at John and Jed and asked, "Did you miss those two Indians on purpose too—just like ya did with me?"

She expected her sass to make Jed's fur bristle like it did the first time, but he looked at her without a word. The man appeared to be as stubborn as a mule and as mute as a stone.

"Let's go have a look," John said. "It's time to get moving anyway."

They gathered their things and led the horses down

the steep trail. It was a tough ascent but even dodgier going back down. John stopped twice on the way, then continued with the reins in his left hand and his rifle in his right. As they descended to the bottom, Jodi saw two dark spots.

It was blood—not just a few drops; it was coagulated and so dark it almost appeared black. A single eagle's feather stuck in the grass fluttering in the breeze. Jodi thoughtlessly picked it up and stuck it in her hatband. Then she followed the men down the rest of the way.

They mounted and rode south at a lope when they reached flat land. Still, nobody bothered to say precisely where they were going or even how long they planned to ride south. Maybe they were headed for Mexico. At least in Mexico, no Texas sheriff or marshal could detain or lock Jodi up. She doubted little the Waco sheriff would forget the ugly cut she left on his face.

All her life, her temper had gotten her into trouble. That wasn't her only fault, though. She was a sucker for the bad boys. She only had a couple of short romances back when the ranch was still intact and her pa was alive. Both men had been in trouble with the law, but that didn't deter the rancher's daughter.

Twice during the day, Noland vanished without a trace. The first time he disappeared, he returned a couple of hours later. Jed didn't offer any reason, and Jodi didn't ask, even though she wanted to. The second time she began to get spooked.

"Is someone following us?" Jodi asked. "We've been riding hard and far. Don't you two ever stop? Why does John keep disappearing every few hours?"

This time when she talked to Jed, he looked at her like he'd just noticed she was there. He almost had a startled look in his eyes. Or maybe he realized she wasn't who he assumed she was.

"You never can be too careful, ma'am," Jed said and almost smiled. "John and I've soldiered together nigh on the entire war. As soon as the captain saw me shoot in training, he took me from my regiment. I figure John must have been with the captain from the first. As soon as I got transferred, John trained me right there on the job. He's my spotter, and I'm the shooter. It's only been just over four years, but it feels like it's been forever."

The man's eyes seemed to drift to some other place before he regained his composure. Then, he looked at Jodi again and snorted like a horse. Until now, Jed's face had been no more than a stone, never making any expression at all. Suddenly he looked more like thirty than thirty-five, and his eyes sparkled a little. When he finally relaxed his face, most of the wrinkles fell away. There was life left there, even though the war left its internal scars.

He showed her how keenly aware he was when he caught her looking at him oddly.

"Why, you're still wet behind the ears," he said and snorted again.

It was like he just realized she was only in her twenties. Now it was Jed who inspected the cowgirl. Her boots were scuffed and worn from wear, much like her saddle. She wore a Navy Colt six-shooter on her hip like she was born with it there. He wondered if she knew how to use it or was she just another sassy woman from one of the pleasure palaces that dotted the west. There were many women made hard by the Civil War. It was a struggle for everybody. Just the same, he considered her no more than a kid, although shapely.

Jed said, "Make sure you don't shoot one of us with

that cannon you got on your hip. I hope you know how to use it."

Jodi tried to act angry, but the anger vaporized like a breath in the winter. Instead, she stared at him like a startled doe. Then, she realized how she was acting and got so frustrated she became angry all over again.

"So, what is it?" Jed asked, finally making some ordinary conversation. It sounded like he hadn't spoken to a woman for a long time. "Your story, I mean. Why are you running with us? I figure if you are willin' to ride with the likes of us, you must be running from something pretty bad."

"A man back in Waco grabbed my butt," Jodi said as the back of her neck turned red. "I waited until he was good and drunk. In the alley beside the saloon, I lured him close enough to thump 'em in the temple when he staggered out. I got my gunsights filed down, so it cut his face good too."

"And?" Jed asked. He knew there was more.

"That and my daddy died. I lost our ranch after they stole all my cattle. The bank took it from me. I guess I am running from a bunch of things."

"What I mean is, is that all you've done?" Jed asked as he stared into her eyes. It was almost unsettling. "Why I thought you killed the governor, something really serious."

"The fella I disfigured turned out the be the new sheriff in Waco. Our ranch was just out of town. The Yankee lawman hadn't even put his badge on yet. If it weren't for bad luck, I wouldn't have any luck at all," she explained.

"Bumping into us might have been your good fortune yesterday, but today may be a different matter. We know the Yankee Army is looking for us, and there's a passel of them. Then, the men we rode with don't take kindly to deserters, either."

"But the war's over," Jodi said. "Didn't everybody just go home? The Confederates, I mean. What else were you supposed to do?"

"First of all, we took off a month before the war was over, but everybody saw it coming. General Lee just didn't wanna give up no matter how much it cost. Many men were of the same spirit. My regiment is from Missouri, and all vowed to fly the black flag and not give up the fight.

"John and I saw things differently, though. I ain't no politician and, hell, John was a slave. Just because Congress says all the slaves are free doesn't mean it's going to happen from one day to the next.

"There'll be resistance and lynching. Many men in the war saw too much and ain't fit for nothing else. For many folks in Missouri, the war started six years before it was officially declared. I doubt it ends any quicker.

"So, besides the Yankees, we might have what's left of the Confederates—definitely somebody from Quantrill's Raiders—looking for us. They'll consider us deserters. Especially John, who both deserted and ran off from his owner."

"What's the black flag for?" Jodi asked, puzzled.

Jed changed again, and his face became impossible to read. He whispered, "The regiments who flew the black flag, gave no quarter. We spared no one."

"I read all about Quantrill's Raiders," Jodi whispered, almost in disbelief. "Some say they were heroes of the Confederacy. The Yankees say they were butchers, and the captain was a devil."

Captain Quantrill's Raiders, Bloody Bill Anderson

Marauders, and Todd's Gorillas had the worst reputations in the South for their viciousness.

Suddenly, Jodi began to have doubts about the men she had chosen to ride with. She wondered if these two quiet men could have ridden with such a man as Quantrill and committed the crimes she read in the newspapers.

Of course, the details depended on the newspaper you read. If it was a Rebel rag, Quantrill's Raiders were heroes. It was a different picture if the paper came from east of Ohio.

Neither man appeared capable of doing what she read in the northern periodicals from New York, Chicago, and Boston. She also read about Todd's Guerrillas, who were apart from the two hundred men who rode under Quantrill.

Out of nowhere, John appeared a few yards away on his horse. Jodi startled, but Jed acted like he already knew he was there.

"I didn't see anybody tracking us other than the Comanche from last night," John said. "No White men, for sure. We can give the horses a rest. At the end of the day, if we can find a safe place, we can make up a hot meal again. Maybe even take a rest for a few hours more than usual."

"I guess your sheriff don't know which way you ran," Jed said as a small smile finally graced his lips and settled into a grin.

"What are you grinning about?" John asked, shocked.

He hadn't seen his war pardner smile for four years. He acted dead serious from the day the captain picked him to be his head sniper. Despite himself, the Black scout felt a smile creep over his face, too, showing his shiny white teeth.

It was good to see Jed smile. Strangely, he looked like another man. He sure didn't look like the killer John knew him to be. He shot countless northern soldiers and nearly always by penetrating enemy lines. When he smiled, he looked like a normal human being.

Just look at that boy now. Who would imagine the things we had to do. Yeah, back then, he was like a different person, and only I know what he's capable of.

CHAPTER 8

THE POSSE

THE THREE FUGITIVES FOUND ANOTHER GOOD LOCATION IN a blind on the top of the hill. At the edge, mesquite trees stood in a line like pallbearers at a funeral. It allowed them shade and cover from a trail that saw more traffic. They had the advantage of cover and an excellent position. Jodi felt so much precaution wasn't necessary, but both John and Jed knew better. Things often went to hell when least expected. Both thought they had ridden too long without encountering an enemy other than a few Comanche. Their flight was just too easy.

In less than an hour, the horses were hobbled and nibbling on clusters of grass grouped around thorny cactus. Flies buzzed around their heads as they flicked their ears and swished their tails. By the time Jodi finished with their mounts, the fire was burning bright and the smell of coffee floated through the air. The cactus plants were thick at the back of the campsite, leaving long black shadows as the sun neared the horizon. It provided a slight respite from the hot day as they rested in the shade.

"So, what did you do before you brained the sheriff?" John asked and chuckled. "You look more like a cowgirl than a desperate outlaw."

"I've been a cowgirl all my life," Jodi replied. She noticed Jed wasn't listening to the conversation. At least, it appeared that way. "We had a sizable spread built up over the years. My ma died when I was born, and my pa never remarried. So, he never had a son. I guess he tried to make me the son he always wanted."

"So, who's runnin' the ranch with you on the run?" John asked.

"The Southern Army bought a lot of our beef. Some they paid for, and some they didn't. We got paid in Confederate dollars. They had no value the day after the war ended. As far as the ranch goes, they pretty much cleaned us out between the rustlers and the Comanche after Pa died. As soon as the war was over, I couldn't pay my ranch hands because my money wasn't any good. So, they all rode off to find employment somewhere else. By then, the bank was selling my land off in plots because I couldn't pay the bills. Things ain't too good in Texas these days. I reckon we should have stayed out of the war."

"I never knew we had a choice—I mean normal folks like us and certainly not slaves," John spat. "We got no say at all."

"It seems to me we all three got thrown into something we weren't looking for," Jodi pondered.

As she looked at the sun near the distant mountains, she thought back on a couple of years before all the trouble started, and they no longer had control over their futures.

"Put that fire out," Jed said with urgency.

He pulled John's spyglass out and brought it to his eye and gazed into the distance.

"You were right, ma'am," Jed whispered. "We've got nine posse members behind us. I can see the tin stars reflect in the last bit of light. It looks like they're pulling up for the evening. They got a couple of Indians with 'em too. That must be how they tracked us here. I doubt anybody but an Indian could follow John on what little track we've left. We're damned careful."

Without a word, John brought his blanket to the edge of the hill where Jed sat, and he passed him his Sharps rifle. The scout pulled a tuft of grass, raised his hand, and let it drop.

"The breeze is maybe three miles an hour from your left," John whispered as they settled down to wait and watch.

When Jed looked through the scope, he could see the men's faces in the last vestiges of light.

"You ain't gonna shoot 'em, are ya?" Jodi asked, alarmed.

"Would you rather invite 'em to dinner?" Jed asked as he peered through the scope. "Come here and have a look to make sure it's the man you walloped."

Jodi threw her blanket beside Jed's and lay down, so their silhouettes didn't show in the outline of the hill. The sun was in their faces.

"Don't push the rifle forward. The scope must stay in the shade," Jed said. His voice was as soft as the breeze. "That way, it won't reflect the light, and they won't know we're here."

"In the morning, we'll have the sun to our backs," John observed, already planning on what they would do and how they would escape.

Jodi lay down beside the sharpshooter, took his gun,

and looked through the telescopic lens. She'd never seen one before. When she looked at the group of men around the fire, they appeared so close; she was startled and pulled her eye away. She looked into the distance with her naked eye and then turned to the scope again. This time, she swept the scope across each man's face.

As Jed lay there and stared at the camp below, he noted the scent rising from Jodi's hair. It smelled of something he hadn't noticed for a long time. She smelled like a woman, like wildflowers and honey. For a second, he almost lost his train of thought.

"Nobody's going anywhere tonight," John said. "We can go out later and have a peek to see how well they're armed. Then, we'll know all we need to plan our attack and escape."

"We might as well eat before the beans are cold," Jed said like it was just another day on the battlefield.

When he pushed himself up, he couldn't help but notice how the denim of Jodi's jeans stretched tight across her bottom. Then he averted his eyes before John saw him.

"That's him, all right," Jodi said. Concern filled her voice and eyes, but she kept a steady face when she looked back at Jed.

"Don't worry, ma'am," Jed said. "We won't let 'em hurt you as long as you're riding with us."

"If we kill them, they'll want us for murder," Jodi whispered and wondered if she got herself into something bigger than she realized.

John and Jed exchanged knowing looks. They knew what they were. They were called 'Bushwhackers' by Kansans, and they already were wanted for murder. To them, a lowly town marshal way out in Texas didn't mean a lot after all they had to do to stay alive. Jodi, seeming like some relic from another time, was helping them both feel more comfortable about life after the war.

Jed remembered the young women he courted before the conflict. Now, that he looked Jodi in the face, he saw how pretty she was in a tomboyish way. He pushed the thoughts from his mind, though. He knew what awaited him in the future. There was no place there for a woman.

Unlike her uncle, Goodnight was as impulsive as hell. She often did things before she thought them out, like whacking the sheriff in Waco with her pistol. On impulse, she joined up with two men from the infamous Quantrill's Raiders. She wondered what the hell she was doing riding down a one-way road to the valley of destruction.

"Let's rest tonight," John said. "We can get up before first light, when they are deep asleep, to check their weapons. We know who the boss is, so that is an advantage."

"How is that?" Jodi asked.

"If you kill the commanding officer first, often the skirmish is either postponed, canceled or they proceed with less direction. Sometimes they turn around and go back home."

"Had I known he was a sheriff, I'd have never hit him," Jodi said. "But I can't see you takin' his life for something I did."

"What do you think he is going to do to you if he and those other men catch you way out here on your own?" John asked. His anger showed at her ignorance. "They'll rape you and beat you is what they'll do. You'll be lucky if you make it back to go to trial. Then they might hang ya anyway. Folks have a way of getting riled up since the war. Sound judgment escapes them."

Jodi just sat staring at the campsite, which seemed far

away. The men looked like the size of insects from where she sat and waited. She didn't get a wink of sleep all that night. The guilt of what was to come weighed heavy on her mind. Neither John nor Jed knew how she felt, but she was afraid to voice her opinion. She felt entirely out of her depth and didn't know where to turn.

Jodi watched as the two ex-Raiders snuck out into the night. They disappeared almost immediately. As they departed, she didn't hear them make a single sound. Both men had branches and brush sticking out of their hair and clothing, making them even harder to see. In the night, they looked like walking bushes. She didn't ask to go because she was afraid of what might happen.

She tried to see through the dark, but the moon had set, and the black curtain was impenetrable. She pulled her pistol and drew back the hammer—the cylinder clicked loud. She heard small animals scurry in the brush but held steady. She had her metal tested before. She fought Comanche alongside her pa and pistol-whipped the odd cowboy for pushing things too far. She was a dead shot with her revolver, too, but never was drawn to heavy rifles.

She felt her heart pounding between her ears as the time came to a crawl. Seconds were like minutes and minutes like hours. It seemed to take forever for the two men to return. The realization struck her suddenly, like a smack in the face. She knew two against nine was no deadfall. What if they got caught? She looked over at Sandy and almost saddled up. She held her ground, though, and waited as she was instructed.

CHAPTER 9

SHERIFF CONAN

WHEN SHERIFF CHARLES CONAN PULLED UP TO CAMP YET another night, he was getting impatient. His face hurt as the sun dried the wound and the stitches pulled at his sunburned skin. He was going to find that damned woman if it killed him. She disfigured him for life for no cause. All he did was pat her ass.

He had eight men who were at least proficient with guns. He believed their numbers and weapons made them too much for the Comanche to approach. They would be after their horses if they were around at all.

All the men were tired, so the sheriff knew he had to keep them focused, or some of them would wander off and head back home as the fire within each of them began to ebb.

The sheriff pulled a handful of tiny pieces of paper from his jacket pocket and dropped them into his upturned hat. He shook it around and offered each man to take a number.

"What's this all about?" Willy Green asked. He was one of the men from the altercation outside the saloon.

The sheriff grinned a mouth full of yellow teeth and said, "For dibs to see who goes first with the bitch that did this to my face."

His drinking partner looked back at the sheriff with greedy eyes. Half of the men pushed forward to see if they could draw the lucky number; the other half were undecided. They joined the posse for fun at first, but now things seemed to be taking a darker turn.

Since they all wore badges, even the reluctant ones eventually took a number. With tin stars on their chests, they felt somewhat invincible, something unnatural to the majority. They believed they were the law and could do pretty much whatever the sheriff said.

"How do we know which one is the winner?" Willy asked as he shifted from one foot to the other in nervous anticipation. He reached up and closed his eyes and grabbed a piece of paper.

"The winning piece of paper says BITCH on it," the sheriff said, his smile flashed evil.

Willy Green opened his and looked, but he appeared puzzled. He turned his eyes to his buddy, the town sheriff, and asked, "What's it say?"

"It says you won, amigo." Conan snickered after he glanced at the illiterate man's chit.

"What about the rest of us?" his other drinking partner asked.

"Don't worry none, boys," Sheriff Conan thundered. "You'll all get a chance. I have no intention of letting that little whore return to Waco. We can leave her for the Comanche when we finish with her. I'll teach her not to mess with Charles Conan. I'm the new sheriff of Waco, Texas, for Pete's sake."

∼

Up on the hill, a cold camp was kept that night. That meant Jodi would have to wait in the dark to protect the horses from Comanche while Jed and John checked out the posse.

"How in the world did I end up here?" the cowgirl whispered to herself. Her mind was screaming for her to flee them all and take her chances in the dark. For some reason, she couldn't do it, though. She set out on her own when she ran out of town. Now, she found herself between a rock and a hard place and with little idea of what to do.

She squatted between the horses with her six-gun in her hand. Every time she heard a bush rustle, her eyes followed the barrel to the sound. She could hear voices from the men camped in the distance but could not understand a word of what they said.

As usual, John led Corporal Coal toward the enemy, just as he had for over four years. They moved forward with slow deliberation. Carefully picking each spot to step, never making any noise to alert the posse.

"Maybe we shouldn't have left the woman behind," Jed whispered. His voice strangely sounded like the breeze.

"Where'd you plan to hide her?" John asked. "She ain't a tracker and can't come with us. Plus, we need her to watch the horses in case the Comanche try to steal 'em."

"That's what I'm worried about," Jed huffed.

John stopped suddenly and looked at his friend and whispered, "For the last four years, we ain't worried about what happens if things go wrong. Now why are you gonna start worrying about a woman you don't even know? I got a hint she can take care of herself. It's good it's so dark. It'll make her and the horses harder to see. Hush up. We ain't got much farther to go."

As they crawled the last few yards through the shadows of twilight, the only hint they were there was the whites of their eyes. Their camouflage made it impossible to discern their outlines. They were close enough to hear what was being said around the campfire.

When they picked the numbers from the hat, John looked at Jed and frowned. They saw they mainly had single-shot long guns and pistols. The handguns would prove useless unless they were at close quarters. That was not in the plan.

They lay there nearly an hour, until they had heard enough and backed out the same way they came. They made less noise than pocket mice as they carefully crawled across the silvery landscape. The twigs in their hair were the only hints of movement.

When they reached the dark camp, both men stopped and listened. They could barely hear the horses shifting their hooves. They realized they would have to enter the camp carefully. They didn't want to scare Jodi. She might shoot them straight off. The gun she carried didn't look like it was used only to smack ornery lawmen on the noggin. It hung low like she knew how to use it.

They heard a horse nicker. Jed looked at John and shrugged his shoulders. They would both back away in a normal situation and wait until daylight so it would be easy to see if the Comanche had arrived and set a trap for them. It also would ensure Jodi would not put a bullet between their eyes. They didn't have the time, though. They heard what the posse planned for the girl, and they were so close you could nearly spit that far. They had no choice but hope for the best.

"What's her name again?" Jed whispered to John.

"Jodi," John replied, but he smiled because he knew damned well, Jed hadn't forgotten.

"Jodi, don't shoot. It's John and me. We're coming in," he said as loud as he dared.

They moved toward the horses and found her sitting between two in the dark. They also found themselves looking down the barrel of a Navy Colt and a small light caliber pistol she must have had hidden.

"Take your fingers off those triggers, girl," John said. "You might shoot one of us by accident."

"Damn, you're full of surprises," Jed whispered as he stared at the second gun. "Are you carryin' anything else we don't know about?"

"Is it really them?" Jodi asked.

John looked at the woman and thought about what he heard, trying to decide how much to tell her. What they had planned wasn't pretty; that much was for damned sure.

"It's them all right," Jed said. "They're a wicked lot, Jodi. From the way he acts, I reckon the sheriff was a soldier. The rest are townsfolk, but there ain't a good one in the lot."

That was the first time he called her by name. It almost startled her when she heard it. It put her off balance for just a second.

"They're just a few drunken men," Jodi replied as she quickly regained her composure.

"No, they ain't," John said. "The plans they have for you be wicked to the bone. Let's get organized, Jed."

Before the sun even peeked over the hills behind them, they were at their respective positions. John selected the order and checked the wind as Jed adjusted the gunsight and settled in. They had the sun to their backs so the men below wouldn't be able to spot them from this distance. Not in time, anyway.

"How do you know which one is the sheriff?" Jodi asked right before the first gunshot rang out.

"We know," Jed said as he reloaded the Sharps rifle in a blur.

Corporal Coal looked down the scope to make sure the first target was down. Now, they would be unorganized. The following shots were at the two trees where they tied their horses. When the limbs exploded and fell on their mounts, they pulled free and bolted from the camp. Jed killed the sheriff and set the posse afoot in less than five seconds.

It was a turkey shoot. Next, Jed aimed for the man who won the prize. Malice filled his eyes as he pulled the trigger, decapitating the foul-mouthed son-of-a-bitch. When they lay there listening to all the terrible things they planned to do to Jodi, his blood boiled with anger.

Jed knew he was a killer and a vengeful man, too. He intended to send every member of the so-called posse to hell where they belonged. He pulled the trigger again, and the other man who huddled with the sheriff dropped with a gaping hole in his chest.

A Sharps rifle can drop a buffalo at two hundred yards and kill a man at half a mile. John called the next shot as Jed moved the barrel of the long gun toward the target.

"STOP!" Jodi screamed.

Both John and Jed looked back at her, puzzled. They didn't know what to make of it. They gazed at her like she was from some other world. Impatience showed on John's face. It wasn't good to interrupt a shooter.

"Spit out whatever it is ya got to say quick," Jed said, "before the rest of this scum gets away."

The wild look in his eyes made her take a step back. Her heart raced in her chest, making it hammer. A blue blood vessel throbbed at her temple. Jed had tombstones in his eyes. She was speechless.

Just the look on her face made Jed take a look at himself. He glanced at John, nodded his head, and they gathered their things without another word. They all silently saddled their horses and continued to ride south. Jed led the way. He rode way out front, clearly wanting to be alone. John watched him go as he had many times in the past.

He knew he had demons inside, like all the men did who went through the hell that caused brothers to kill brothers and fathers killing sons. In the end, the war made little sense to Jed. But it did to John. As he chose such a life, he knew he would never reap the benefit that would slowly come. But some of his family would.

His destiny was already written in stone, as was Jed's. They both knew it and didn't deny it. It was a hard thing to admit to others, though. There were no words for what they did and what happened to them and theirs. There was nothing more divisive or vicious than Civil War.

CHAPTER 10

SAN ANGELO

WHEN THEY GOT SAN ANGELO IN SIGHT, THEY TURNED right, down a dirt road full of potholes and water puddles. Deep wagon wheel ruts snaked their way through the fields. It rained throughout the morning, but the sun was out again, chasing away the dampness and bringing healthy rays of sun. They navigated the trail, which looked like it had been the target of a battery of cannon. When they got to the end, they came to a small, impoverished village. As soon as John saw the little shantytown, he grinned from ear to ear. They had finally made it, and he would get to see his family after many years.

A million questions hammered John's mind. His brother lived here, and he hadn't seen him since they were young. Their plantation owners sold them to different farms. That was where John learned to shoot a rifle so well. He was the plantation master's gun handler and accompanied him on hunting trips for pheasant and quail. His tracking game and marksmanship skills prompted his owner, Mr. Francis Asbury Noland, to loan him to the Confederate army.

Like many slaves, he got his owner's Christian name, but he was never set free. He loaned him out to Quantrill to scout for his Black Flag Missouri Raiders. Of course, nobody ever asked John if he wanted the job or not. He went where orders dictated, even if it was into the valley of death.

After fighting in the Confederate army during the last years, he hadn't felt so much like a slave as he did a soldier. When men's friends die in each other's arms, it erases color. Men see each other's souls. John bonded with Jedidiah. He was as good a friend as he ever had, and he never treated him other than an equal—even as a wiser elder on occasion.

There wasn't another White man alive he would bring here. John wasn't even sure he should have come. Time would tell if he was welcome or not, or if his presence would present a danger for his family. Post-war America was in total turmoil, and one never knew what they would encounter.

Jed stood beside John, and Jodi hung back in their shadows. The presence of the White woman had completely slipped Noland's mind.

A man walked out of the house. The building had clapboard siding and a tent roof. The floor was covered in planks to keep them dry. Jed was shocked the brothers looked so much alike. He never imagined another John walking the world—but there he was. They were like two peas in a pod. Jed turned around almost as an afterthought and saw Jodi shyly standing behind them.

"Come on over," Jed said. "We won't bite."

Jodi still remembered the look on Jed's face when he killed the sheriff and his men, so she was reluctant at first. Once her eyes met his, her resolve vanished like a spring shower, and her mind pushed the violence back into some dark corner. She beamed when Jed smiled, and her heart skipped a beat. She felt drawn like a magnet to the rough-looking soldier. She knew he was damaged goods, but she had already felt the attraction. She wondered if he felt it, too.

As John met with the last three living members of his family, Jed and Jodi patiently sat and listened. They were the last known members of his family because some were sold off and never heard from again.

They had a quiet reunion. Jed's brother, Jim, was set free after the Civil War—only some months back. He still hadn't adjusted to the difference. Most of the plantations lost everything. Businesses built on Confederate dollars held vast fortunes, which were lost overnight.

They didn't have the money to pay for laborers once the slaves were freed. Some slaves turned on their cruel owners to exact revenge. Others were simply hung or murdered by pro-slavery whites. The South was on fire, and the future looked bleak. At least in Texas, three outcasts were on the edge of the violence. If they traveled farther south, it might even be safer.

The first night was full of drinking and introductions. The family and a few friends reminisced about their childhoods on the second day. Jed and Jodi found themselves alone for the first time since their worlds collided.

Jed was seated in a chair with his legs crossed and his hat off; it hung on his boot. A cheroot dangled from the corner of his mouth as he stared into space. Lightning bugs lit here and there, making their nightly dance while mosquitos buzzed in their ears. The air smelled like freshly cut hay.

When Jodi walked over to a chair next to Jed's, he didn't appear to notice. She sat down, and he didn't say a word. His eyes were open, but it was as though he wasn't there. Jodie wondered what occupied his mind. She saw the look before on several occasions over the last days. It was like he remembered a time before he changed into the man he was. It was as if he was beckoning for his old self to return but to no avail.

"Are you really related to Charles Goodnight?" Jed asked out of the blue.

"I said I was, didn't I?" she replied smartly and then bit her tongue. She was so accustomed to being on the defensive, the sass came out all on its own. It was as though her thoughts did what they wanted, and words walked right out of her mouth with no will of her own. "I didn't mean it that way."

"Didn't ya?" Jed asked. Then, he smiled, and his face suddenly changed because his eyes smiled, too.

It was like night and day. All the things he had seen in the war seemed to drop away for just an instant. That was all it took for Jodi to know, though. She knew inside the dangerous rough exterior lived a gentle and kind man. She was never so sure of anything in her life. That was when it hit her like a Baldwin locomotive. She was falling in love and, like always, with a bad boy. Jed was no boy, though. He was a full-grown man.

She seemed doomed to fall in love with men who were bad for her, but she couldn't resist. This time she surprised herself because he was quite a bit older. She never had a beau who was more than ten years her elder. As suddenly as the realization hit home, so did doubt. What if he didn't like her? He never gave her any indication she was even alive until now.

Since the day he shot the sheriff and those other two

men, they'd hardly talked to each other. It was as though they were avoiding the inevitable confrontation. She didn't intend to bring it up either. She preferred to commit her thoughts to his handsome smile.

"I never see Uncle Charles all that much," Jodi said. "I ain't seen 'em since the end of the war. He served here in Texas for the Confederacy but mostly fought Indians in the frontier forts. He's a big shot rancher. So, he's always on cattle drives. His ranch is over five hundred acres. He's planning to drive three thousand head of Texas longhorns to Montana. He's going with his friend, Oliver Loving. Can you imagine that? They could take the better part of a year to make it that far, not alone getting back home."

"That's a long way to take a herd of cattle," Jed said. "I come from farmland myself. But that was a long time ago. It feels almost like another life. Anyway, I reckon half the state of Texas has heard of Mr. Goodnight. Some say he's what's called a millionaire."

"How much is a million?" Jodi asked as crickets chirped and she watched the flashes of light in the night.

"I can't even imagine so much money," Jed replied. "Me, I'd prefer to live the simple life of an unknown man." He seemed to drift off again, but added, "If I had a wish, that's what I'd wish for."

Jodi wasn't about to let a sad conversation ruin her first time to talk to Jed. "Let's go for a walk," she suggested.

"You wanna go for a walk?" Jed asked. "We've been walkin' for days."

"Well then, let's go for a stroll," Jodi said, making her eyes twinkle enticingly. "Please? I heard you say you were a gentleman. So, do a lady a favor and humor me."

Her smile spread so much it hurt her jaws when Jed consented.

They strolled the opposite way they came in and, within five minutes, they were out of the shantytown and on a country road. Deep shadows marked the landscape. Jodi took off her hat and shook her hair loose. For the first time, Jed noticed how long it fell down her back. Her blue eyes looked black in the moonlight, and her lips the color of blood.

At the end of Jed's cheroot, the cinder fired bright as he puffed billows of smoke. They came to a small pond and watched as the moon wavered on the water's surface. Jodi had to control her breathing as her heart raced and the blood thundered through her body. Although Jed didn't appear to feel what she did, she could sense the energy building between them.

Why doesn't he kiss me?

Jodi waited breathlessly, sensing it was going to happen any minute.

"We best be getting back, or they'll wonder if we didn't run off or somethin'," Jed said, much to Jodi's disappointment.

"What?" she replied as her bubble burst. Suddenly she was brought back to the harsh reality of where and who they were.

The war-worn soldier just turned and chuckled. She skipped a couple of steps to catch up. She felt it again, but she could see he didn't. Jodi wasn't going to give up just yet, though. She decided at that moment she would do whatever she had to do to get him to pay more attention to her. She longed to for the chance to show him who she was. She doubted the war had spoiled his chance for love. She had heard of such things happening.

She knew a lost soul when she saw one, though, and Jodi intended to do what she could to lessen the suffering that held his heart hostage.

CHAPTER 11

PICNIC

THE FOLLOWING DAY JOHN NOLAND INVITED HIS PARTNERS to a family picnic. Though his family was dirt poor, the two ex-Confederate soldiers had a small cache of money. One of the differences between regular Southern soldiers and Quantrill's Raiders was they kept their victims' spoils. The captain, originally an Ohio school-teacher, turned a blind eye to such thievery. He felt it only befitting the victors reap the rewards. It helped teach the Jayhawkers a lesson, even though he never participated.

Nobody knew why William Quantrill joined the border war. He came to the western frontier and continued to teach in local schools. Hidden inside this mild-mannered educator was a tiger and, in many eyes, a villain.

It was hard to explain in simple words. Few men experienced such a conflict. Some towns were at odds with the next village. People who never had differences before and had known each other all their lives now sought to kill each other. Brothers fought brothers and fathers battled sons. There were Bushwhackers or Jayhawkers, and nobody could sit on the fence. Residents had to pick a side or end up an enemy to all.

Bloody Bill Anderson had differences with Quantrill when they wintered in Texas in 1863. Bill left the captain to ride north, organize his marauders and told the local sheriff Quantrill was an outlaw. The captain was temporarily arrested and jailed, but he soon got out.

He had two hundred harden men riding under his black flag. Bloody Bill was so extreme in his violence, he soon became the most famous of the Raiders. This mattered little to the captain, though. He was fighting for a cause. Quantrill thought Bill Anderson was no more than a bandit and killer.

In Missouri, many people sided with the Raiders and thought they were fighting for their state rights. Others saw what they did as an atrocity. Jed and John were swept up into the whirlwind by no decision of their own. Sure, Corporal Coal signed on as a regular soldier, believing he was fighting for the South. He never owned a slave, so he never quite understood that part of states' rights. Noland understood it all too well, though. After years of fighting, a day in the country was a welcome deterrent for everyone, even those with newfound freedom.

There was a fishing pond nearby with good shade and crystal-clear water. Going on a picnic was a simple thing for most people. It was all new for John's family. His brother and their cousins were enslaved until the last days of the war. Similarly, Jed and John had just left the fighting and were still trying to get beyond it.

They both believed San Angelo was not far enough south for them to stop their flight from certain punishment and death, though. It would be easier to track

John's brother down than the outlaws themselves. John and Jed had secretly discussed the situation early that morning and decided it would be best to be ready to flee at first sight of danger.

Today, though, they all forgot about the past and turned their eyes to the present. Each one appreciated a moment of peace in the wicked world in which they lived. They forgot all that happened for a few hours to give them some respite from their daily toil.

Of course, none of the plantation owners paid their slaves, and John's brother still hadn't found work. Some of the people were talking about something called *crop-sharing*. In the end, it was just another way to continue slavery and make it legal in the eyes of the law.

It was Sunday, and that was as far as they allowed their minds to drift. John rented a buckboard wagon from the local stables, and his cousins rode in the wagon that was chock-full of picnic surprises. Jed and John gathered all their belongings, including their weapons, and rode apart.

When they were still preparing to leave, Jodi looked at John and asked, "Are we leaving for good? I thought we were going on a picnic." Her eyes twinkled at the prospect.

John stopped for a moment, as though Jodi's question caught him off guard.

"We ain't gone nowhere for four years without all our kit because we never know when we're gonna have to escape or fight."

"Do you think today is going to be dangerous?" she asked and snickered softly. "We're going for a picnic, boys. Relax for a spell. It's only for one day."

As usual, Jed never even looked her way. It was as if he wasn't even listening to what she said. He seemed to permanently be in a world of his own, waiting for him and his scout to go work. They were like two men joined at the hip.

John looked her right in the eyes and smiled as he strapped on his revolvers and grabbed his Henry rifle.

If the truth be known, they carried their weapons for so long they felt utterly naked without them. They sure as hell didn't want them somewhere else if they were to need them suddenly. They'd been in the Army for too long not to know danger and violence could come at the most unexpected moments.

Even though Jodi was prickly at their reaction, she begrudgingly packed her things too and strapped on her Navy Colt. It seemed far too large for the petite woman until she pointed it at you. Then, it got ugly fast. She generally pointed the barrel with a rock-steady hand.

When they pulled the wagon up to the pond, it was about eleven, and the morning sun shone gloriously. The smell of nature was everywhere. The sun slanted through the leaves of the trees like rain. The tinkle of the spring talked as it flowed over stones and filled the pond. When the sun kissed the flowers, they turned their faces to the morning heat.

Dragonflies bounced on puffs of air just above the water's surface. Sugarcane grew all along the far end of the pond, making it a natural home for fish. You could hear the long stalks whistle in the breeze. On the other side, cattails bent while tiny ripples of water scurried across the small pond. They saw water boils on the surface where fish fed on insects. Occasionally a bass would break water and splash.

Jodi sat on a rock by the bank, pulled off her boots and socks, and rolled up her pant legs. She walked to the edge and stepped into the water. Mud squished through her toes as the cool water brought relief.

Tiny frogs with their tadpole tails swam clustered at the edge as they flashed under her feet. Occasionally the bright-orange side of a carp would surface lazily. Catbirds flittered in the tree overhead, making their raspy mew sound much like a feline.

The men got busy unloading the wagon. They brought chairs and a small table which soon was covered with home-cooked food. There was a basket of fried chicken, a stack of Johnny cakes, cornbread, cornmeal mush, black-eyes peas, collard greens, mashed potatoes, sweet potatoes, sweet tea, and two pies. One was a shoofly pie, and the other was a peach cobbler. They brought a large ceramic jug of corn whiskey to help them relax and spend a lazy day eating, drinking, and fishing.

"Have you ever been fishing?" John asked Jodi.

"Is snow white?" she asked and chuckled. "I'll go dig some worms and see if I can find some caterpillars. Maybe I can get some from this tree we're shading under."

"There's a small spade in the wagon bed," John replied, smiling.

Jodi jumped up, grabbed a low-hanging limb, and nimbly swung into the tree. The catbirds fled as the White girl climbed higher until she found what she wanted. Dozens of catalpa worms nibbled on large leaves. She filled her peach can with the live, bright green, squiggling bait. Below John had already grabbed the spade and dug in the soft dirt beside the pond. He filled another can with long, fat night crawlers.

By the time Jodi climbed down, the men already had cane fishing poles in their hands and a fried chicken leg in the other. Four red floats bounced in the middle of the pond, and the two soldiers sat on a flat rock on the bank with their bare feet dangling in the water.

"Nightcrawlers, you say." Jodi smiled and grabbed a catalpa worm from the can.

She pinched its head off then used the hook to turn it inside out. When she had the bait on the hook and tied on the red cork, she swung the line back and forth until she got enough momentum to toss it toward the bunch of sugar cane on the far bank.

When her float hit the water, it went under but didn't even bob back up. She immediately saw a catfish run for the shelter of the sugarcane with her hook in its mouth. She fought hard as her cane pole doubled under the weight.

She pulled it to the bank, then tossed her pole down and pulled in the fine string. Finally, she grabbed the catfish while being careful to avoid the spines on its back and sides. She strung one end of a rope through the fish's gills and mouth as it thrashed in the water for freedom. She tied the other end to a small stump so it wouldn't work loose. In just five minutes, she had a handsome catfish on a stringer.

None of the Black men or the soldiers got a single nibble. Their floats lay still in the water as though not a single fish lived in the pond.

"What did you say you used as bait?" John asked, curious. She was the only woman in the group, and she was out-fishing them all.

"Caterpillars from the catalpa tree right above you. I've never found a better bait."

Jed sat on the far end of the rock staring into the still water, but she couldn't tell if he was listening or not. He appeared to be content just by sitting uninterrupted. Even John sensed his mood and left him alone.

Jodi was having the time of her life, though. She was putting the men to shame at fishing, something that didn't go well with John's brother and cousins. Not until they tried her secret bait.

John pulled his worm off his hook and fished around in Jodi's can for one of the green squiggly caterpillars.

"You've got to pinch his head off first, then set the hook into its tail and turn it inside out on the hook," Jodi said. "There ain't a fish in Texas that can resist such a morsel. Lucky for us, it's summer because they're only around in June and July."

John drew the fishing pole back to his side and swung it across the pond. His float sat in the water as still as a stone. He waited for a few minutes, but nothing happened. Then the float disappeared but bobbed right back up. It happened a half dozen times before the hook finally set. Whatever was on the other end was big because John's fishing pole nearly doubled to his waist.

He was sure it was going to break, but it held. They were all rooting for John and had forgotten entirely about the war. Even Jed watched as the other Black men rooted John on. When he got it near the bank, Jodi jumped right in, grabbed the line, and drew it closer hand over fist.

She let out a yelp when it was three feet from her and jumped back.

"Give me some rope, quick," she shouted. "We got a snapping turtle on the line."

The cowgirl nimbly made a lasso on one end, and she looped it around one of the turtle's feet and pulled it to shore. It fought like the dickens. The monster held its mouth open and snapped at its captor. It got a hold of

Jodi's pants leg, and she let out another yelp but held fast. The damned turtle was half as big as her. Jed jumped into the knee-deep water and helped pull it up onto the bank.

Jodi grabbed a stick from the ground, and as soon as it got near the turtle's mouth, it clamped down on the wood, nearly breaking it.

"Cut its head off while I hold the stick, John. Don't let go of that rope, Jed, or it's likely to get a hold of me."

The scout pulled a machete from the wagon and lopped the head off the reptile with a single stroke. Its powerful beak released the stick, but the headless animal continued to snap at anything that neared its jaws.

"We're gonna have a mighty fine supper now," John said and laughed. "Turtle soup and catfish. Maybe we'll get lucky and get us a carp. Ain't you gonna try some of Jodi's bait?" John asked Jed.

Jodi didn't give Jed a chance to reply. She grabbed his pole, changed the bait, tossed it in the water, and passed the rod back to Jed. He looked at her like she was from some other planet. She carried on just the same. Almost immediately, he got a strike. The floater raced across the surface of the pond at a furious rate. The fish on the other end of the hook was big and angry. It made a wake in the water as it raced across the pond toward the safety of the sugar cane.

Jed fought the monster for the better part of ten minutes before they pulled the massive carp to the shore. Jodi grabbed a branch, quickly pulled her knife, and hacked a sharp point. Then she jumped into the water, speared the massive fish in the side, and tossed it onto the bank. It flipped and flopped as its shiny orange, blue, and yellow sides sparkled in the sun.

"Lord have mercy," Jim said. "That's the biggest carp I've ever seen. What did you call them worms again?"

When Jed looked at Jodi, he did so with a slight smile on his lips and life in his eyes. He, too, was beginning to enjoy the day. That dark cloud that perpetually floated over his head momentarily disappeared, and the sun sparkled in his eyes. The Jedediah Coal that was hidden deep inside the-torn man was beginning to emerge. Not so surprisingly, Jed suddenly looked twice as handsome to the cowgirl.

Soon, all five were tugging at fish for all they were worth. Soon they had three stringers full of fish dangling in the water from the tree stump. A dozen fishtails flipped and flopped in their attempt to break free and escape. For once, escape was the farthest thing from the minds of John and Jed.

CHAPTER 12

SUDDEN CHANGES

THEY ALL LAUGHED AT THE MESS OF FISH THEY CAUGHT
and passed around the jug of corn whiskey. Jodi slipped
her finger in the hole and flipped it on her elbow. Next,
she tilted the heavy jug up and took a long swig. She
pounded on her chest as the fiery liquid burned its way
down her throat, and a tiny burp escaped her lips.

She giggled and said, "Excuse my poor manners,
gentlemen, but I am a country girl."

It was obvious Jodi tried to forget what Jed did to the
sheriff who chased her. Right now, she only focused on
the fishing hole and the picnic. It was one of the first
days she enjoyed herself since her father died. The jug of
moonshine made its way around the circle until it was
empty. It left everyone with a warm, glowing feeling.

In the distance, they saw an old donkey heading their
way at a quick trot. One of the little Black children who
lived in the shantytown was on its back, flaying it with a
short branch. As he came closer, they saw his eyes
looked like saucers. He appeared to have seen the devil.

John's brother, Jim, stood and waited for the bad

news; there was never any good news for people of color. There could be no other reason for the boy to rush to them. When young Amos pulled the panting donkey to a stop, he was so breathless he couldn't get the words out as he stuttered and stammered.

"Slow down there, son," John said. "What's the problem?"

"There's Union soldiers at the house asking about Jim's brother. I reckon that be you, Mr. Noland."

The faces in the small group of picnickers all soured at the words Union soldiers. Once again, the wolves were biting at their heels.

"What did you tell them, boy?" Jim asked, giving him a reassuring smile.

It only made sense they would track down his brother.

"I told 'em my uncles were fishing, and they'd know more about such things than me," young Amos said. "I played dumb. Are they after you, Uncle John?"

"White men always be after Black men," Jim said as he looked at his brother.

A sadness erased the joy on his face. A hardness returned to Jed and John's eyes, making them suddenly look dangerous. It was as though in a second, they were transformed. The Black scout took his brother aside for a moment as they whispered their goodbyes. John shook his brother's hand, and, without another word, he and Jed saddled up their horses.

Jodi didn't intend to wait around to be questioned by the Army just in case they came by way of Waco. She, too, saddled up Sandy and sadly mounted. Jed and John tipped their hats to their friends and family and turned their horses south again and rode off at a lope.

Jodi followed uninvited. She believed they were

giving her a chance to cut herself loose from them after hearing the news. She was going to stick to Jed Coal like glue, though. If the Union soldiers found out she was with men from Quantrill's Raiders, she could only imagine what they would do to her. It didn't matter.

As the two ex-Confederate soldiers trotted away, she turned her horse south and shot off like the devil was chasing her, and maybe he was.

Suddenly danger was everywhere. The quiet, fun day fishing was cut short, just like John warned. They needed to be ready at all times to flee or fight. It was just beginning to sink in. She wondered what they would do now that the Army knew they were in Texas.

Jed looked back and smiled again when she caught up, but the smile didn't reach his eyes. His eyes were tired and weary again, but behind that was a wave of anger she hadn't seen before. It was as though he was suddenly back in the war. With the Union army on their tail, she realized the war was not over just yet.

"You ain't as smart as you look," Noland finally said after they had ridden for over two hours. "I thought you'd be clever and skedaddle once you heard the Yankees caught up with us."

Jodi looked John in the eye and replied, "If I ain't scared of two of Quantrill's Raiders, why would I'd be scared of some Blue Coats?" she said and tried her best to put on a brave smile. It didn't quite make it.

"I fear they'll be hard on my brother," John huffed. "I hope he hid like I told him, so they don't find him. I guess they located him through my owner, which means he's still alive. That's just another nail in my coffin."

Jed brought his horse even with Jodi's and stared down his nose. "If you stay with us, it won't be just to watch like you've done so far. They'll be bringing the war to us, and if you're with John and me, you'll be marked, too. Much more than you are now. Hell, I doubt a court hangs a woman for walloping an ornery sheriff in the noggin for being discourteous. You'd have better chances on your own. You can always say we kidnapped ya and forced ya to ride with us as a hostage. There's still time to save yourself. Understand, though, there ain't a lot of time for thinkin'."

"What about the dead sheriff and his two friends?" Jodi asked. "I reckon they'd hang me for taking part in killing them."

"Not if we kidnapped you," Jed said. "I'm sure the Yankees wouldn't have a problem believing we'd be so nefarious. The newspapers made us out as devils as it is. I reckon some of us were, but not all."

"In the South, you were heroes," Jodi continued. "We could try to find some sort of group of sympathizers, couldn't we?"

"No, not after the Raiders declared us deserters," Jed said. "Mind you, with the war over; I imagine there be tens of thousands of deserters wandering around the countryside. Things are gonna get very dangerous on the trail soon, not to mention the Army's on our heels."

"Hopefully, they didn't catch Jim, and they didn't find out where we're going," John said. "They'll know we've been there, though. The neighbors would have told them a White man and a Black were in town. All the folks in the shantytown knew who we were; they just didn't let on. Just knowing we were there is a problem. The question is, do they have a tracker as good as me? If he ain't up to the task, I may trick them into going the wrong way. At least for long enough to get a lead on 'em. We've got to find someplace to make our trail vanish."

"Hoofprints vanish?" Jodi asked, puzzled.

"Have you ever seen hoofprints in a river full of water?" John smiled. "We're goin' swimmin'. We'll follow the Concho River east until we find a spot with heavy foliage. First, we'll walk the horses into the water like we're heading west, though. Once we're in the middle, we got to force our horses to swim along the river as far as we can before we look for a tricky spot to climb up the bank. If there's lots of foliage, all the better. It'll be easier to cover our tracks. They won't know which way to go at first. So, either they'll split up or decide a direction. Whatever they do, it'll give us more time."

When they reached the river, Jodi was glad her mare liked the water and wasn't afraid to swim. She wasn't nearly as scared of the river as she was the Union army. They had no idea of how many soldiers were following them.

They dismounted and continued in the same direction, walking their horses. It made them appear to keep their original path. When the water was too deep for the horses, they veered into the middle, where the current was more robust.

"Get in the water and let your horse drag ya along the side," Jed yelled. "Grab your saddle horn and hold on for dear life! Use the reins to guide your mare."

The river didn't look like it was moving fast until they got to the middle. Then the current drew them along, and the undercurrent tried to pull them under. The horses squealed and groaned, but they swam on.

They knew the Union army was hot on their trail. It only made sense they would follow in one of two directions. They could either go south for Laredo or west toward El Paso. Then again, they could head for Mexico. Jed and John spoke no Spanish, so they figured they would take their chances in Texas.

CHAPTER 13

OLD OAK TREE

As soon as they pointed the horses toward the muddy banks of the river, they got a second wind and swam for their lives. All three fugitives kicked their feet to help break free of the current. The first horse slipped to its knees as its hooves lacked traction. Then the iron horseshoes dug in, and each one of them powered their way up the bank.

The humans weren't fairing as well as the animals, however. They felt like they swallowed half the Concho River. They crawled up the slippery bank made worse by the horses. They clawed the mud to pull themselves up to the vegetation that began at the very edge.

They followed the path the horses forced their way through. After the animals found high ground, John and Jed used machetes to cut long cane stalks and stuck them into the bank where they exited the river. Then they lay freshly cut stalks covering the entrance to the new path. Camouflaging their exit path, would make it difficult for their pursuers to catch them unless their scout was someone special. Jed was good, but few men could track as well as John. If the Army's Indian scouts could follow them, they would know how to cover tracks too. Time would tell.

As they sat near the river in a small clearing, the horses shook off the water, and the three outlaws scraped the mud from their faces. Jed and Jodi were as black as John. The humor wasn't lost on the old tracker either. He laughed—then Jodi began to laugh too. Finally, Jed was laughing with them.

Once they caught their breath and the nervous laughter ceased, Jed said, "You know we can't keep on running. If we do, we'll lead them to where we're going. Short of crossing over to Mexico, I don't see us riding any farther south until we do something about that cavalry patrol behind us."

"I'm all ears if ya got an idea on what to do," John replied. "The land's too damned flat here. All we have are a hill here and there. It's getting harder to hide."

"I know what we need," Jed said. He stood in his stirrups and used his hat to shade his face from the sun as he peered into the distance and said, "I see what I want. Follow me."

The three rode off at a lope toward more flat land. They were close to the river, so the ground was healthy and green. They rode across a wide stretch of grassland with few trees, except for one giant oak. Jed looked up and chose the limbs he would climb. It was high enough to give them the advantage. The oak was massive, so it would make it difficult to spot the shooter, at least for the first two or three shots.

"We need food and water for a couple of days," Jed said as he chose the limb they would use for the ambush. "If they have any information on us, they'll come carefully. If not, they'll come all arrogant, like they own the place."

John grabbed his water, some jerky, and hard biscuits. Then, he turned to Jodi and said, "Take the horses south and wait until...on second thought, leave our horses a mile south, and you run for it. We'll find 'em."

"Sure, so the Comanche can catch me and make me a squaw," she snapped back. "I ain't in jail yet, so I reckon I'm free to do whatever I want. Tell me what you've got planned. Don't just send me off with the horses like I'm some fool. Let's get this plan on the table."

Both men looked at her hard, but she was determined. Her right hand hung on the handle of her revolver. It was clear she wasn't going to budge. The woman had a wagonload of grit and was as stubborn as a mule.

"We can make some hammocks between those limbs at the top with some hemp webbing we carry. We used trees to shoot from during the war," Jed said.

"And you're just gonna shoot 'em?" Jodi asked, shocked. "I thought you had some kind of plan. That ain't no plan at all. And you call me the fool."

"You sure are a sassy woman," Jed replied.

"Call me what you want, but even I can come up with a better plan than that."

"Well, we're waitin'," John replied.

"Sounds like your plan is to shoot as many as you could before they overran your position?" Jodi asked.

"No, we were gonna shoot the officers first to see if they turned," John said. "If they didn't, we plan to kill all of 'em we can."

"You'd have a bee's nest of soldiers dying to shoot you. Even if you managed to kill all of them, Lord forbid, then they'd send a platoon instead of a patrol. You would have signed your death certificates."

"What would you do?" Jed retorted, almost angry.

"Whatcha, figure they got? One lieutenant, a sergeant, and a corporal?"

"If it's just a patrol, yeah," John said.

"Then it's simple," Jody said as her eyes sparkled. "We shoot their horses."

"That don't solve nothin'," Jed said. "They'll have extra horses with 'em. I doubt they get a scratch falling off their horses, but it'll help feed the local Comanche. Some say they're suffering the effects of the war just like us."

"How about if they're runnin' flat out, holus-bolus right for you and John. If you shoot the horse and it tumbles, the rider will be thrown. He might even get trampled. Them officers won't be up and around for a few days if we get them at a gallop."

"How do you figure you can get them to take such a chance?" Jed asked, curious.

"How far can you shoot that rifle of yours?" Jodi asked.

"I shot my targets a couple of times near on a mile out, but they weren't moving. Maybe half a mile with no problem at all. There ain't a breath of air, and the sky is clear. At full gallop, you say?"

"Yep," Jody said. She crossed her arms and kicked her hip out, showing her impatience.

"I can do it," Jed said pensively. "Why?"

"I figure Sandy and me can hide in the brush until the patrol shows themselves in this flat bit of land. Just before I'm in range of their Winchesters, I jump on my horse and hightail it toward this tree we're standing under. I'll lead 'em right to ya."

John and Jed looked at the woman like she must have

come from the moon. What she said made perfect sense, although risky for her.

"I don't know about you trying to outrun the Army boys," John said. "The north has money, and the cavalry officers ride good horses."

"There ain't a horse in Texas gonna beat my Sandy in a sprint." Jody smiled. "Whatcha say, men? You told me I wasn't to sit and watch anymore. I'll ride south and drop all three horses off and come back on foot."

"I thought you were gonna race out in front of the cavalry and get 'em to chase ya. Are you gonna do it on foot?"

Both Jed and John chuckled. Even though things were bad, Jed was still smiling then and again. John thought maybe the young filly was good for Jed.

Two days later, they were all three up in the tree. It was the coolest place to wait. The limbs were fat and many, so they built makeshift hammocks to rest and watch. Jodi went back at night to stay with the horses. Of course, she was scared sitting there all night long, hoping one of the horses didn't nicker.

Late on the second day, they saw a cloud of dust rising in the distance. The soldiers rode toward them in double file. There were twelve men plus the lieutenant. Just as expected, they rode like they owned the place.

Memories of the war flashed in Jed's mind. He had hoped to never see a Blue Coat again. It felt strange to meet the enemy again in such a faraway place. He had always fought in Kansas and Missouri.

He suddenly realized their plan would be a hard nut to crack. They were committed, though, and had to go forward with Jodi's plan. God help them if it didn't work.

No matter how well one planned, something unexpected always can affect the outcome. It was a throw of the dice, but so was life. Maybe today, they would be lucky.

The cowgirl whistled for her mare which came running. She led her into the high grass where Jodi kneeled. Her cow pony wasn't much higher than the shrubs they hid behind. She rubbed Sandy's nose, whispering soothing things to her. Inside, Jodi felt like her head would explode with her heart thundering in her ears. She clutched the reins with white-knuckled fists. Just a little farther now. If she ran too early, the trap would backfire, and they would have to fight it out before it launched. If she ran too late, she was in range of a dozen rifles.

Initially, her idea seemed brilliant. Now, she wondered if she had erred, believing she was somebody she wasn't. She sure did hope Jed was worth it and as good a shot as he claimed.

Her shrill scream startled John and Jed. It was so piercing and high, it sounded like someone was killing the woman. It shocked the patrol, too. It stopped for just a moment. Jodi removed her hat and used it to slap Sandy's rump as they ran for the oak tree. Just like she planned, the soldiers all broke into a neck-breaking run.

Jed took careful aim at the lieutenant and pulled the trigger. His horse's legs collapsed, and the rider was thrown head over heels onto the hard ground. He lay there and didn't move. John got sight of the sergeant and led Jed to the shot. Another report and a second rider went down, but he sprang back up, holding his shoulder and howling. They guessed it was broken.

Surprisingly the corporal rode with a pack of five young soldiers and they continued the chase, oblivious of the fact the officers had been injured. The last five pushed their horses hard; they panted under the strain. John spotted the sergeant, but Jed saw two more men in front of him, and they were gaining on Jodi. He took a bead on the first rider hoping his shot would dismount one or both.

He fired, and the horse dropped. The corporal made a full face-plant on the hard-packed trail. He rolled and tumbled. Blood gushed from his nose when he rolled over. The horse nearest him spooked and bucked in mid-gallop, tossing its rider high into the air. Miraculously, the horse kept its balance and ran off like the forest was on fire.

At the last minute, not a hundred yards before the oak tree, the patrol pulled up. The horse that tripped over the corporal broke a leg. So, they shot it. At least the local Comanche would have plenty to eat for the next few weeks. Maybe even a few settlers would be sustained. Horse meat was as good as beef to folks who were starving.

CHAPTER 14

UNCLE NOLAND

It was before sunrise and a chill had set in. Jodi stirred from her bedroll, got up, wrapped her blanket around her shoulders and squatted before the growing fire. She rubbed her hands near the flames. John was getting supplies out to make breakfast. He looked over and saw the woman's silhouette against the light. Jed still was resting quietly.

The night was a rough one. Not so much for the Black man, but Jed's nightmares disturbed Jodi. John warned it was dangerous to wake him during such torment. Somebody tried once and nearly got shot for the effort.

The odd thing was John knew exactly what the nightmares were. He was there in Lawrence, Kansas on the morning of August 21, 1863. They rode with Captain Quantrill and Bloody Bill Anderson as company commanders.

Two companies, totaling four hundred fifty guerrillas, were heavily armed. Some carried as many as six revolvers. Each man had years of experience and a grudge as big as the sky. Both sides had been at each other's throats for years.

Lawrence had bragged it could defend itself against up to five hundred Rebels, but it wasn't true. Everything came to a head that day. Men died. The newspapers said it was the worst massacre of the Civil War.

For Jed, it was more than he could endure. The nightmares started a couple of weeks after the incident. He woke up half the camp.

There were young boys fighting on both sides. The youngest man in Quantrill's two companies was Riley Crawford. He was only thirteen. That morning they assembled outside Lawrence before first light. Before nine o'clock, they had killed one hundred fifty men and boys. Some of the children were as young as Riley, maybe younger by a year or two. Many of them wore remnants of Union soldiers' clothing and were armed. At the time there were more than 100,000 Union soldiers who were fifteen or younger. Toward the end of the war, boys were sent to fight. The youngest Union soldier was an eight-year-old drummer boy in the 22nd Michigan. He was wounded at the Battle of Shiloh. His name was John Lincoln Clem, but his peers named him Johnny Shiloh after the battle.

That first evening of nightmares were the most harrowing. Nobody knew what Jed might do or how he would react if awakened suddenly. When they finally tried, he immediately reached for his knife and gun. John wrapped his hands around the barrel before he could pull the trigger.

Some nights were worse than others. Jodi found it hard to sit by and do nothing. John saw mixed feelings in her eyes.

Of course, she was scared. Hell, the first dozen times,

it scared the daylights out of John. With time, he hoped Jed's mental wounds would slowly heal. The scout was fifteen years older than Jed. It made him feel more like his uncle than his friend. The things they had witnessed would make most men faint.

John Nolan rolled a fallen log over beside the fire and sat before a pot of vegetable and beef stew. The aroma wafted through the air as he stirred it with a wooden spoon. His face was clouded in vapor making his expression hard to see.

"How is it you make dinner for breakfast?" Jodi asked.

"We got used to making the healthiest meal at the beginning of the day in case we didn't get a chance to eat again. It gives us the energy to go through the day without stopping until supper. We often had to make cold camps, so you made a good meal whenever ya got the chance. War is hell, ma'am. Especially this one. It was bloody beyond imagination."

They sat for a spell in silence. The only sound was the wooden spoon scraping against the bottom of the metal pot. The sky blushed red as the sun graced the world yet another day. Cirrostratus lay like wisps of hair across the blue sky. Jodi sat beside John and sighed. He smiled at her.

"You be too young to be so mixed up, girl," John said. "You've only made the one mistake, unlike Jed and me. I reckon we've had this all mixed up from the beginning of the war."

"But you didn't sign up of your own free will," Jodi said. "You were forced to do what you did. Jed didn't volunteer to ride under the black flag either. Y'all ain't like the others. I've read about the James brothers and the Youngers. Read about Bloody Bill Anderson and Captain Quantrill, too. It's all been in the newspapers, you know."

"Oh, I know all that," John replied, "but Jed don't. I don't know why but some men are affected differently than others. Oh, I have my days as we all do, but Jed has some deep scars inside. It's funny he didn't get as much as a scratch after all that. Hell, they shot me three times."

"Should I wake him?" Jodi asked.

"Lord have mercy, no. Let him sleep. He's been fighting his demons all night. He's tired. I know his demons personally, and they're many."

John turned and studied the young lady for a moment. He dared look into those blue eyes. He nodded his head as though he just understood something he hadn't before.

"Is Jed married back in Missouri?" Jodi asked as she stared at the flames and not at John.

The scout glanced at her for a moment; then he began to laugh. He immediately covered his mouth with his hand to keep from waking Jed.

"No, ma'am, I don't recollect him ever being married," John replied as he stirred the stew. "Or if he was, they all be dead. I remember him tellin' me his farm and crops burned, but he had little more to say about it. He claimed he had nothin' to go back to."

"Jed ain't the most talkative man I've met," Jodi said. "Why does he ride off all the time like that? It seems every time I say something to him, he runs away."

"You be right. Jed, a talkative man? No, that he ain't," John replied as he stared into the steam produced by the stew.

When Jodi glanced up at the former slave, the cinders

from the fire reflected in his eyes. Just for a moment, they looked red and demonic. His smile revealed he wasn't haunted by demons like his friend, though.

John stopped stirring the stew and turned his head to look at the blue-eyed woman. A grin spread across his face.

"What?" Jodi asked. She stared so hard at John her eyes nearly crossed.

"You've takin' a fancy to Jed, ain't ya?"

A blush the color of cherries rose from Jodi's neck to her cheeks. John completely caught her off guard. She was waiting for him to say something, but was surprised when he did. Jodi knew it was obvious to everybody but Jed. She'd have to run him over with a team of mules to get his attention.

"Is it that easy to see?" Jodi asked, breaking eye contact and looking at her boots. She rubbed a tiny hole in the dirt with her toe.

"I reckon not, ma'am," John said. "I only noticed just now. Then again, we ain't talked that much."

"To tell the truth, neither one of you is much at talking. Jed's as mute as a tree stump."

The earth turned on its axis as the sun orbited the globe, again rising into the sky. Heat began to make things waver in the distance. To the west, black storm clouds gathered, forming a dark mass. The world was divided in two. One was full of light and glory and the other dark, rumbling and foreboding. The atmosphere matched how Jodi felt inside. She felt like she had one foot in something that could be wonderful and the other on the path so dark she couldn't see the train for the tunnel.

Distant thunder began to rumble as bolts of lightning shot from one dark cloud to another. Jed yawned, threw his blanket off and rubbed his eyes with the heels of his hands. He sat up and eyed the two of them seated on the log. He pulled his revolver from under his saddle and slipped it into his holster. He stood up and strapped on his gun belt. He almost looked embarrassed.

He felt like he was hungover and hadn't slept a wink. He didn't remember what his dreams were about, but he was aware he had them. He wandered over to the fire, and John passed him a cup of coffee that was thick as mud and kicked like a mule.

Jodi seemed broody and Jed slightly embarrassed. John took it all in stride. Life was always hard for a slave. He never had any expectations of better things. So, he always made do with what little he had. Only folks who lost something they owned felt they had something coming to them. Folks who never had anything knew better.

Jed scratched his growing black hair and rubbed a two-day growth. His mouth was dry as dirt and his eyes were red and tired. After two coffees, he began to wake up. The transformation was visible as he shrugged off his demons until they came to haunt him the next time.

"How much farther south are we gonna run?" John asked as he scooped a spoonful of stew into his mouth.

"We're almost to Laredo," Jed replied. "If we ride any farther, we'll be in Mexico, and we don't speak the lingo. We could stop for a spell. If we don't like it, we can ride west for El Paso or maybe even Arizona; it's a divided state. Men from both sides come from Arizona."

"Do you think they'll be looking for a White man and a Black man?" John asked. "I'd reckon by now all of Quantrill's Raiders are wanted."

"Hopefully, they won't be looking for two men and a White woman. Maybe you'll come to be a benefit, Jodi,"

Jed said. "We best think up a story and get it straight before we walk into any town. The war just ended a few months ago. People will be suspicious of strangers. I saw a lot of men riding south, and they weren't goin' on no picnic."

CHAPTER 15

LAREDO, TEXAS

THEY RODE INTO LAREDO WITH JODI IN THE MIDDLE. SHE pushed her hat back, so it was obvious she was a woman. Not that any ordinary man with a pair of eyes would see anything different. She seemed shapelier than when she first joined up with John and Jed. Or maybe the way Jed looked at her had changed. John was amazed his partner had actually conversed with the woman for the last three days.

They weren't long conversations, but he was talking. Jed used to mope during the war because he couldn't share his thoughts. John knew he had to communicate to heal. Nonetheless, Jed never shared even with him, and they spent nearly every hour of every day together the last year of the war.

When Captain Quantrill suspected the war wasn't going the way they wanted and the government funds were low, he got desperate. He sent Jed and John on countless missions to target Yankee sympathizers or Union soldiers. One was as bad as the other to the captain. Any man who disagreed or fled, was shot in the back by the mild-mannered schoolteacher from Ohio. It was a threat the captain repeated to his men frequently.

So, they did as they were told. They killed anyone, man or boy, who carried weapons. There were a lot of boys fighting on both sides due to the shortage of men. The Raiders even torched businesses and houses.

John and Jed set limits on what they were willing to do in the name of the cause. They never killed unarmed children or women. So far, they'd been lucky. A stray bullet never went that way.

The main street was bustling as they rode into town. Wagons were stopped at general stores and haberdasheries, unloading their goods. As they walked toward the saloon, Jed stopped midstride.

"We all fancy going in and having a drink, but we don't know if they'll let John in or what they'll think of you?" he said to Jodi.

"I don't care what they think about me," she replied, grinning. "I can take care of myself. You two hold on, and I'll go on in and ask the proprietor. Here in Texas, being polite and showing good manners goes a long way."

Before either man could object, she was pushing her way through the batwing doors. When Jodi walked into a room, the men's eyes always looked her way. In part, it was her strappy nature. Then, there was the fact she was a damned good-looking woman, even if she did appear to be a few years older than twenty-six.

Behind the bar was a disheveled man with a dirty apron. It hung from his neck down past his knees. He wore scuffed boots, but his grin was pleasant, and his eyes kind.

"Howdy, young lady. What can I do for you?" he said.

"I come with some friends," she said, then hesitated,

"and one of them is a Black man. Is it all right with you if he comes in and has a drink with us?"

"If you've got money, pay in advance, and don't start trouble, you're welcome in my saloon anytime. My name's Justin Burrs. The Lone Star Saloon is my place; I make the rules."

"That's mighty kind of you, sir," Jodi replied and raced back out to get the boys.

"Come on in, gentlemen." Jodi smiled. "We're perfectly welcome as long as we behave ourselves."

When they walked into the dim saloon, Jed and John eyed the few patrons, remembering where every window and door was. In the corner sat three men with beige hats. When Jed saw the stars, his heart nearly stopped.

"Are those Texas Rangers?" he whispered.

Jodi looked over their way and said, "I wouldn't worry much about the Rangers. They didn't have to fight the war because of the border problems with the Comanche and bandidos. We needed 'em more down here. Most of 'em are Southerners anyway, but they got their hands full without sweeping up the mess left by the Civil War. Their war started decades ago, and they'll still be fighting twenty years from now from the looks of it."

Since Jodi seemed happy with the situation, Jed and John tried to relax, despite the fact they were sharing space with a bunch of Rangers. When the three lawmen finished their drinks, one walked toward the bar and the other two stood waiting by the door. When he got close, he slipped his cover over his wavy hair, and he turned his stare to Jodi and tipped his hat.

He turned back to the barman and asked, "How much for three beers and three whiskeys?"

"They're on the house, Ridge." Justin beamed. "Just

make sure you send Rowdy, Toby and the boys when they get off work."

"Are you trying to bribe me, Justin?" Captain Creek asked as his eyes narrowed. Then, he laughed and threw a double eagle on the bar. "The boys' drinks are on me tonight and don't forget to keep my change. See that Clinton ain't carried out of here in a wheelbarrow like last time, too."

Before stepping outside, he turned and looked at the three strangers at the table. It was like he was memorizing their faces for the future. Jed held his stare for a moment. His eyes looked like those of the dead men he had shot. It was unsettling. He turned and left, the sergeant and corporal following.

Despite his bravado, Jed let out a sigh. "Did you get a look in that man's eyes? Lord, they were scarier than Bloody Bill Anderson's."

"The Texas Rangers are a hard bunch," Jodi said. "But they're not interested in us. They already have their hands full and only a few people to do the job. There ain't but a few dozen Rangers on the frontier."

By the time Justin brought them a bottle of whiskey, three beers and three bowls of steaming hot chili and bean soap, they were ready to eat a bear. About halfway through their meal, eight more Texas Rangers arrived. Most of these were young except an old fellow. He looked like the oldest Texas Ranger alive. But they kept to themselves and drank heavily since the drinks were on their boss.

There was still plenty of daylight. So, the three newcomers fancied a walk around town after a few drinks and a meal. Jed and John hadn't walked in a town that wasn't war torn in a long time. Jodi just enjoyed the company. As they walked down the streets of Laredo,

Jodi grabbed both men by the wrists and dragged them inside a haberdashery.

"It's high time you two buy some decent clothing," Jodi said. "I can't be going around with you two dressed in rags. Your shirts and britches got holes in them. Go and find the man in charge."

An hour later, the three walked out, and they looked like different people. Jed wore a black suit just like John. The most surprising change was in John's appearance. He was allowed a uniform made up of bobs and bits while riding with the Confederates. But he wore cotton pants and a jacket. He also bought a new hat. It was a black felt Reiner. John sported a new pair of brown boots with stars stitched into the sides.

Jody stuffed her jacket, shirt, and denim pants into her saddlebags and walked out with a revealing white dress with leather trim. Her six-gun looked natural on her hip. When she passed other men, they turned their heads to look. Strangely, Jed felt he didn't like her getting the attention of men like that. Jodi saw it in his eyes, too, and flaunted it. She realized, even though he felt it, he didn't even know what jealousy was.

The trio's mood was high-spirited, what with full stomachs, that fuzzy feeling from a few shots of whiskey and new duds. All three felt like a million bucks. They walked nearly to the edge of town. As they strolled down the boardwalk, their boot heels hammered on the timber planks. Across the street, the inebriated Texas Rangers were staggering back home.

Jodi pointed out the Texas Ranger Post as she walked between the two finely dressed men. A tall, lanky man was pushing one of the Rangers in a wheelbarrow. All of them were dead drunk and armed to the teeth. The three outlaws were happy they had gone along on their way.

Lawmen with a gut full of whiskey and lots of guns were often dangerous. Jodi recalled her incident with the sheriff and the saloon in Waco.

Suddenly they heard dozens of hooves hammer the street. They saw an Army patrol pull up in front of the Ranger headquarters. Ridge Creek, the man they saw in the saloon, walked out to greet them.

"Damn, the jig's up," Jed whispered. "Act natural. They shouldn't recognize us in our new duds. John, step into the alley until we see if this is about us or not."

They watched as the lieutenant gestured wildly. He was almost shouting, but they couldn't understand what was being said. When the Ranger pointed his finger in the direction of the Lone Star Saloon, Jed said, "Shit! You see that, John? The Yankee lieutenant is talking to that scary Ranger."

They gritted their teeth, expecting the worst. Nobody heard what was said, but suddenly Ranger Creek was wrestling the lieutenant's horse to the ground. He grabbed the bit and bridle and pushed it backward, so the bridle sunk the horse's nose to its chest. He twisted the horse's neck until it threw the Army lieutenant to the ground.

Finally, he pulled his pistol out and thumped the Blue Coat on the side of the head. The officer's fur bristled as he staggered to his feet, but a dozen Rangers armed with heavy Colt Walker revolvers stood behind their boss. A stream of blood ran down the side of the lieutenant's face. This all happened in a few seconds.

Beside them, they heard somebody stifle a chuckle. When they looked, it was an older man with a beige hat and a Texas Ranger badge, but he looked too old to be a Ranger.

"Ain't the captain a card?" he asked as he slapped his

thigh and cackled like a hen. "I bet a dime to a dollar that fool officer sassed the boss or insulted him somehow. Captain Creek looks poorly on sass and bad manners. He won't tolerate it! I reckon y'all gathered that."

He snickered some more to himself and took the last puff on his hand-built cigarette, threw it in the dirt and ground it with his boot. Then he scuffed his way across the street with a cloud of dust in his wake.

The desperados turned down the alley and walked as casually as possible for the livery stables and their horses. Once again, they were on the run, and the wolves were biting at their heels.

When they got the liveryman squared away and their horses, they mounted and headed northeast along the border.

"I reckon that crack on his noggin from that gun barrel should give us a few hours head start," Jed said. "That gun looked like a cannon. He was staggering badly. I'd pay a double eagle to know what the Yankee said to the Texas Ranger."

"I wonder why that Texas Ranger thumped him like that?" John pondered. "I ain't seen many men stand up to Army boys. It almost seemed unprovoked it happened so fast."

"Whatever it was that caused it, just be thankful it happened," Jed said, "or we'd have the whole patrol after us. How many soldiers did you count, John?"

"Eight or nine, I reckon," John said.

"There were ten counting the officer," Jodi said, sure of herself. "There was a captain and a sergeant, but he had his arm all wrapped up. I reckon he was the one that fell so hard from his horse."

"We should have shot 'em when we had the chance,"

John said as he looked at Jodi. She was the one who wanted to spare the men instead of killing them."

"Don't worry; I'll come up with something to do. I'm always full of ideas," Jodi said, her confidence over-flowing.

Jed and John exchanged doubtful looks, but Jodi didn't see the change in their eyes. She seemed to be having the time of her life. Suddenly she appeared to be relishing being a wanted outlaw. Who would have thought a cowgirl from Waco, Texas, could be so ornery? They had no better plan, so they let her keep talking about what they should do next. They were both used to taking orders but not from such a scrappy woman.

By the time Laredo was out of sight, the sun had begun to set over the horizon like it was hanging from a string, still deciding to set or not. Bright yellow and orange rays streaked the hills. The sun finally set, and the moon rose on the opposite side of the world. The atmosphere's moisture magnified it; it looked orange like a pumpkin.

Black shadows disappeared from the trees' western side and cactus; silver shadows appeared on the eastern side. They had plenty of light to travel safely at a lope at night, especially if they followed the road where there was no resistance.

They doubted, with the thrashing the Army officer received, he would be traveling that night. Jodi, Jed, and John rode into the sunset and carried on all night. They rode by the light of the moon and stars. It gave them just enough visibility to pick their way across the lunar-looking landscape. The silver orb seemed suspended in the sky as if by magic.

"We got to stop for a spell," Jodi said.

Both men pulled up with questioning eyes. "What is

it?" John asked, and he tried to see in the distance behind them.

"I can't ride any farther in this damned dress," Jodi stated smartly. "I've got to get back into my riding clothes. I don't want to ruin my new clothes either. I would suggest you two do the same. I haven't had the chance to wear a dress since my pa died. Hell, I didn't have it on an hour, and we had to up and run again."

John looked at Jed, puzzled. Until today they hadn't even considered how they looked for years. Hell, as a slave, John never had any say in what he wore. They both did as they were told, though. In ten minutes, they were all riding comfortably at a lope along The Rio Grande and in Comanche country.

They hesitated to ride on the south trails that Jodi said weaved along the river. Those were the trails the hostiles used to make raids over the border on nights just like this one. They rode on until the moon was just inches away from the end of the world. Jodi took the lead and steered them toward a large tree upon a more prominent hill. It was visible from the main trail.

They rode to the top and under the shade of the tree the desperados stopped. There was plenty of grass under the tree's canopy, and they let the horses loose to get their fill while they could.

"Come on and grab that machete and help me cut some branches," Jodi said as she pulled some hemp twine from her saddlebags. "Give me your fancy duds. Don't worry; I won't ruin 'em—I hope."

When they finished, there were two stick figures dressed in gentlemen's clothing. They looked like two more men from a hundred yards with the fake figure's backs to the valley.

"Now to add the final touches," Jodi said. "Jed, climb

up in that tree and set up your shooting hammock. If they're following us, they'll be coming the same way we did."

Then she made up a noose with a loop of rope she had tied to her saddle and threw it over the lowest limb. She slipped it over John's neck, catching the old scout off guard.

"Get this noose off my neck!" he grumbled as he pulled at the rope.

"You don't think I'd hang one of my only friends, do ya?" she asked. "If the Army does show, we want them to see me tying your hands and feet like I'm fixing to hang you. If I know the minds of Yankee soldiers, he'll come a running to put a stop to yet another lynching. Then Jed can do his business."

"Now, you want me to shoot them soldiers?" Jed asked, confused. "Why didn't ya let me shoot 'em before?"

"We were just giving him a last chance." She smiled. "I reckon he already used up all his wishes. It's time to put that bunch chasing us to sleep."

As Jed strapped his rifle over his shoulder and reached for the lowest limb, Jodi grabbed his hand and said, you don't have to kill 'em. Just wing the lieutenant and the sergeant good, and they'll head back to Laredo for a doctor. By then, we could be anywhere. Make sure they won't recover too quickly. I'd rather not have them on our tail again."

They hobbled the horses on the back side of the hill and let them graze where they wanted. They also made a small cookfire to make up hot coffee for the wait.

They didn't know if it would be a day or two, but they believed the soldiers would feel they had to pursue now that they were so close. Hopefully, they would fall for Jodi's trap and then give up.

CHAPTER 16

LIEUTENANT PICKET PIERCE

ONCE THE PAIN SUBSIDED FROM THE SERGEANT'S BROKEN collarbone, the Army headed straight back out after the last of Quantrill's Raiders. Sergeant Lenny Luis had his left arm tied tight around his body. Despite his injury, his superior officer insisted he accompany the patrol. Luis never questioned an officer's order in his life, and he had no intention of starting with something so minor.

They had made fools of the patrol so far. After they killed the Waco sheriff and two of his deputies, wanted posters of Jed Coal and John Noland were distributed to every Army post across the frontier.

Lieutenant Picket Pierce had no intention of stopping the chase over a bit of water and a river, though. He was hell-bent on being the man to take down the Missouri Marauders and make a name for himself in the Union army. Pierce believed he nearly had them cornered.

They rode south for days as their Indian scouts disappeared and appeared at a whim. Their constant vanishing was something the officer despised. They had kept him on the path of the fleeing outlaws, so he chose to ignore their peculiar manners. When the scouts suddenly appeared on either side of the officer, he was startled. This was the third time they spooked him, and his anger got the best of him.

"You're both fired!" Lieutenant Pierce roared. "I believe we can find Laredo on our own. From there, we will take our chances."

"You've gotta pay us first," Tuc, grumbled with his terrifying face. His voice sounded like distant thunder.

This was the first time the officer heard him talk, and the Tonkawa Indian seemed even more perilous when he spoke. It was like his voice came from the darkest depths of hell.

"Fifty dollars is what you said you'd pay us," Potak, the Tonkawa medicine man, added and smiled.

"But we haven't caught the outlaws," Pierce retorted arrogantly. "I'll pay you half."

Tuc nudged his horse in front of the officer, blocking his advance. He repeated in a voice from the grave, "Fifty dollars."

His mouth was no more than a gash and his eyes were ablaze with violence. Pierce had never seen a man with such a dangerous presence, and he immediately folded.

"Pay the heathens," Pierce ordered his sergeant and tried to avert eye contact with the evil-looking warrior. "Give them their fifty dollars and be done with them."

Sergeant Luis pulled two double eagles and a single eagle coin from his pouch and passed them to the Indians. Potak accepted the coins, put them to his teeth, and bit each one, making sure they were real. Then, they seemed to glide across the country without another word until they again vanished without a trace.

"Those are two of the strangest Indians I've ever seen," Lenny said. "I don't fancy using them again, boss. I'd hate to meet up with that Tuc alone in the wilderness."

They were finally to the border when they rode into the town of Laredo. The streets were abustle with activity. The lieutenant stopped and asked for directions to the sheriff's office. When they pulled up, he ordered his men to dismount and wait in the shade by their horses.

He didn't intend to waste too much time with a local sheriff. He only wanted to know if anybody had seen the fugitives, who now were riding with a woman. He wanted her, too. He suspected she was a southern spy. Why else would she run like she did and team up with such violent men? She had to be another Confederate outlaw.

Pierce stepped down from his horse and walked up to the sheriff's office door. He rapped his knuckles on the door and listened. He immediately heard some grumbling from inside the office. When the sheriff opened the door and saw the Army officer, he slammed it again right in the lieutenant's face. The officer heard a dead bold slide.

From inside, he heard a voice say, "Go away, we don't want any."

"What do you mean you don't want any?" Pierce snarled. "You haven't heard what I want yet."

"I don't have the time to deal with Yankee soldiers," Sheriff Deets called out. "Go down the street and talk to the Texas Rangers. They're law, too. Just tell Captain Creek, Deets sent ya. You'll find the post at the end of the street right on the way out of town. Either that or go to Fort Macintosh and deal with your own kind. I'm busy."

"I demand you open this door at once!" Pierce screamed, furious.

"Don't y'all come into my town threatening me!" Deets yelled back. "I ain't got no time for Yankees. I'm a local sheriff and not a marshal. Like I said, go and see the Rangers. We got enough taking care of our own troubles without looking for more with some fancy Blue Coats."

The lieutenant tried the door latch, but the sheriff locked it from the inside. He just shook his head and decided the sheriff must be a Confederate sympathizer who refused to help the Union.

Hell, he's supposed to be the law. He sure don't act like it.

"Let's go find the Texas Rangers," Lieutenant Pierce ordered his men. "That old goat isn't going to open the door. What has happened to the law in Texas?"

What Pierce didn't know about Texans was they didn't like anybody telling them what to do. It didn't matter if they be from the North or the South. This was Texas, and it was a world apart for those who didn't live there. If a man came talking sass in south Texas, he was likely to end up on the wrong side of a fight.

Passersby gave the patrol directions to the Ranger post. They said it was at the edge of town like the smart-ass sheriff said. The lieutenant became angrier by the minute. He hated the fact he had to deal with the Texas Rangers, whose reputation wasn't much better than Quantrill's men as far as he'd heard. Everyone knew about their unforgiving and violent natures. Even with the warning, he didn't realize with whom he was about to become involved.

The twelve-man patrol pulled to a stop at the lieutenant's command in front of the Laredo Ranger post. Several men sat lazing around, passing the hot day in the shade on the post porch. Some of them appeared neutral to the presence of the northern soldiers, and others already looked unfriendly. They dressed like a bunch of ruffians. The only uniform the lieutenant could see was the matching hats and stars. Apart from that, they wore a miss-matched variety of clothing in various states of wear.

What they all had in common was lots of guns. Most of them had a brace of Colt Walkers. It was a handgun with the extreme power of a rifle, especially at close range. Many of them had third and fourth pistols shoved down their belts and boots. They all wore large Bowie knives, and there wasn't a friendly face in the bunch.

"Who's the man in charge here?" Lieutenant Pierce asked with more arrogance than needed.

They all saw how the Union officer looked down his nose at them. One man was levering the handle of a green pump. A few stood at the side of the building, pitching pennies up against the wall. Five more sat in various states of relaxation on the porch. They were all eyeing the intruders menacingly.

A tall man sat in the back with his chair tilted against the building. He pushed his beige hat back with two fingers as he rolled the cheap cheroot from one side of his mouth to the other. He seemed unimpressed with the small patrol of soldiers. Texas Rangers and Union boys often didn't see eye to eye, especially when they weren't Texans. They were from northeast somewhere by the ring of the lieutenant's accent.

He pushed himself up and off the chair and took three steps onto the side of the porch. Captain Ridge Creek spat his smoke out and turned his dead eyes on the officer. He saw him flinch.

Creek gave the slightest hint of a sardonic smile as he said, "You must be lookin' for me."

"I am Lieutenant Pierce, and you are?"

"That depends on the what and why," Ridge Creek replied.

"What do you mean it depends on what or why?" Lieutenant Pierce retorted, getting angrier by the moment.

"It's a simple statement. What is it you want me and my men to do?" Creek asked. His voice lowered and sounded more dangerous.

Uncertainty showed in the lieutenant's eyes despite his effort to hide it. A dozen Rangers stood, ready to defend their boss.

"I'm Captain Ridge Creek and this is my post. Now, what the hell do y'all what? We just came off the trail from rousting a bunch of Comanche and don't feel like being bothered. So, spit it out."

"I am hunting two deserters from Quantrill's Raiders," Pierce replied. "One is White about thirty-five, and the other is a Black man and is supposed to be about fifty. Last we saw them, they were with a woman, a Confederate spy."

"How can she be a spy if she's in Texas?" Captain Creek asked. "There ain't no Yankees to spy on down here, except maybe y'all. I heard a woman of your description talkin' in a saloon earlier. She was as Texan, as I am, Lieutenant. She was with a White fella and a Black man, though."

"Just tell us where you saw them—please," Lieutenant Pierce replied with sarcasm. He was out of patience and found the locals as uncouth as the heathens.

Ridge pointed down the street and said, "Head that way three blocks and turn left, and ya can't miss it. It's called the Lone Star Saloon. Tell Justin Burrs I sent ya. I saw them there this afternoon, but I ain't seen 'em since."

"Finally, a decent answer from you bunch of nitwits," Lieutenant Pierce said as he prepared to turn his horse and head for the saloon. He couldn't resist insulting the sorry bunch of losers.

Captain Creek didn't take well to sass, though. He grabbed the bit of lieutenant's horse with both hands and pushed its head down till it touched its chest, and then he twisted the horse's neck until it dumped its rider in the street.

The soldiers put their hands on their rifles, but suddenly found themselves looking down the barrels of two dozen Colt Walkers and not a shaky hand in the bunch. When the lieutenant stood, already beginning to insult the captain some more, Creek pulled his pistol in a blur and bashed him alongside the head, again dropping him to the ground.

Ridge Creek stared at the patrol, daring anybody else to disrespect him. None of them wanted to confront the ill-tempered Ranger boss.

"Sergeant Weston and Ranger Clinton, escort these men to the saloon and then directly out of town," Captain Creek ordered. "Take a couple of boys with ya just in case they change their minds and wanna stay."

"You can't treat an officer of the United States Army this way," the lieutenant bellowed as he pushed himself up on one knee.

"Oh, who says I can't?" Creek snarled. "I'll try to remember that if you are fool enough to come back. But I can't guarantee anything as I have a habit of forgetting things I don't give a damned about. Be forewarned, though. Next time, I won't be so gentle."

The captain turned his back on the officer, walked over to his seat, sat back down and leaned his chair against the wall. He pulled his hat down over his eyes. It was clear the meeting was over.

The soldiers acquired fresh mounts from Fort Macintosh which had been occupied by the 2nd Texas Calvary since the end of the war. They knew they needed to head northwest before the outlaws crossed the river, or they lost them in the vast stretches of West Texas.

CHAPTER 17

THE LYNCHING

AS THE LIEUTENANT LED HIS MEN FORWARD, THEY KEPT their eyes peeled, knowing how well Coal and Noland could shoot. They'd learned their lesson, but that didn't stop them. They had orders to clean up the last of the Missouri scum, and he felt nothing but a growing need for revenge. He wasn't sure what they would do, but he knew their strengths and weaknesses. He believed the woman would slow them down.

When he finally caught them, he would either hang the men or stand them before a firing squad. As far as the woman was concerned, he had yet to decide her fate. He would have all the Rebels cut to pieces and thrown to the wind if it was up to him. The Army demanded a certain amount of protocol, even way out in the wilderness. All he needed was for one man in his patrol to report an atrocity, and his career would be over. It was odd. Just a few months ago, Union soldiers were encouraged to commit atrocities. Now, they had the eyes of the newspapers on them; they had to follow the rules. War was hell, and Lieutenant Pierce believed there should be no limits.

The lieutenant pulled up, stood in his stirrups and pulled his hat low to shade his eyes. In the distance, he saw four silhouettes on a small hill under a tree. He pulled out his field glasses and put them to his eyes. He frowned when he saw what looked like four men preparing to hang a Black man. They already had a noose around his neck and appeared to be tying his hands and feet.

Hangings had been going on in the South since the war's end. Some slave owners believed their property had no right to be freed, and violent confrontations arose between whites and blacks. Lynch parties were becoming commonplace all across the South.

"I'll be damned if I'm going to stand by and allow Confederate supporters murder innocent Black men on my watch," Lieutenant Pierce said. "Let's go stop this atrocity immediately."

He raised his binoculars one last time to his eyes and watched a man tie the feet of what he clearly saw was a Black man. He couldn't see the other faces, but their color was just visible. He was sure the other three were White. He nudged his horse into a trot and moved with his men up the hill.

"What are your orders, Lieutenant?" Sergeant Luis asked. "We can handle these Rebels while we're at it."

"How about we let the Black man free and hang the three southern scums," Corporal Slade Jones said with a hearty laugh. "That'll get their goat." His laughter sounded evil.

"I would have felt better about this if we had scouts to reconnoiter, boss," Sergeant Luis said.

The sergeant looked up at the hill and found it

strange, lynching a man in broad daylight. Usually, they did this type of deed at night. He had an uneasy feeling, but he always followed orders to the letter.

"Do you know where those scouts are?" Lieutenant Pierce snapped. "Every damned time I look, they've disappeared again."

"You fired them, sir?" Luis said. "I paid them off. Remember?"

"I knew I shouldn't have hired heathens. They're nothing but trouble. Both of 'em were just young bucks anyway. What the hell are they gonna tell us at their age?"

"With all due respect, they say they be the best scouts in Texas," the sergeant replied. "Tonkawa Indians make the best scouts in the west, sir. They're at odds with all the tribes, so they side with the Whites for the most part. We can't trust other tribes, and I couldn't find a White man willing to hunt down Rebels with the Comanche out here. Everybody's at everyone else's throats since the end of the war."

"Bugler, a skirmish line at once," Lieutenant Pierce called out.

A quick burst of notes came from the bugler, and twelve men fanned out and formed a long line. They advanced as one toward the rise in the land and the tree with the noose hanging from a low limb. As soon as they saw his column of soldiers, the lieutenant knew they would either run or give up, but they wouldn't be hanging a Black man this day.

Pierce was a true northerner from Columbus, Ohio. He was a long way from home, though. Before the war ended, he'd often wondered if he'd ever return. He knew he soon would be walking the streets of his hometown.

With the war over, there still were a few things to tend to first.

He was also aware the Army could change his plans at any moment. He had personally entered into combat with Quantrill and his Raiders because they had killed many Union soldiers during the war. It left him with one last score to settle. No one could doubt the viciousness of Quantrill's men.

The report said he, too, was from Ohio. The lieutenant wondered how a schoolteacher from the Buckeye State could wind up in the middle of Missouri leading such a merciless band of marauders.

He heard Quantrill returned to Ohio as soon as the war was over. He walked off thinking he'd just go back home and resume everyday life as if what he did never happened. He was mistaken.

Lieutenant Pierce prided himself in being the man to roust the captain and chase him to Kentucky. A few of his most loyal men fought an entire morning, but Pierce had fifty battle-hardened soldiers with him. They had no chance, and the lieutenant wasn't taking prisoners. That was just a couple of months ago. As soon as he heard more than forty of the Raiders ran south for Texas, he hand-picked a patrol and caught the train south as far as it went and took pursuit on horseback. Picket Pierce was a driven man.

Among the list of ex-Raiders was Jedidiah Coal and a slave by the name of John Noland. They were a sniper team, believed to be running together. The Black man was supposed to be Quantrill's personal scout, and he rode nowhere without him. He wondered why they broke up. The Black soldier would have fared well if he was heading north.

A White man and a Black man traveling together

after the war stuck out like a turkey in a flock of geese, so he went for the ones easy to spot first. He had no idea where the woman came from and wasn't interested in her unless he could prove she was a spy. He didn't think women should be participants in the war. Too many men would be reluctant to shoot and kill a female.

He rubbed the egg-sized bump on his head and felt his anger rise. His neck and face blushed red as they approached the site of the lynching.

As the line of Calvary rode up the hill toward the tree, they were surprised to see two of the figures were stick figures dressed to deceive. The other two ran and took cover behind the large tree. One of them was a Black man. Then, it suddenly dawned on the lieutenant. It was like something you wanted to take back but couldn't. He glanced left, and right as concern filled his eyes. He knew it was a trap.

Lieutenant Pierson turned toward his bugler to give him orders, but he wasn't beside him as he should be. When he heard the first report, it was too late. The second came so quickly after the first it surprised him. The men to either side of him fell in seconds.

He had grabbed the handle of his saber and was preparing to draw it when it happened. Suddenly, he found himself looking up at the sky. Small white clouds drifted across the heavens as Lieutenant Pierce took his final breath.

When John opened fire with his repeater, Henry rifle, men began to drop like flies. Jodi started to fire rounds at the men climbing the hill with her pistol. A flash of fire and a puff of smoke followed her bullets as they peppered the soldiers and their horses. The Calvary was in utter chaos without a leader, falling one after another.

The lieutenant and the sergeant were already dead, as

was the corporal. They were the first men Jed killed. With no leader, the soldiers spun on their mounts with their weapons drawn but nowhere to go. They all began to shoot at the tree's base, where the White girl and Black man hid. Well-placed kill shots continued to rain down on the soldiers, from the tree, though. Finally, the shooting stopped. The sound of flies replaced the gunfire. Soon they would come in droves, as would the rest of the scavengers.

Three vultures already floated in lazy circles above them. Two more sat in trees nearby, anticipating the coming feast.

The leaves above Jodi and John shook, and Jed came crashing down, landing on his feet. He had his rifle strapped over his shoulder. His face was drenched in sweat and his breathing heavy. It was a close call because the soldiers made it much farther up the hill than he had planned. They vanquished this patrol, but Jed and John knew more would follow.

As Jed looked on, he remembered Jesse James. John said he heard Frank and Jesse talking about robbing banks and trains. The talk of robbing a train was just foolish. Nobody had ever figured out how to stop a locomotive. But banks were a different matter.

"If we're gonna get chased like outlaws, we might as well act like outlaws," Jed said. "It can't make things any worse than they already are. If we robbed a bank and got away with, say, thirty thousand dollars, that'd be ten thousand dollars each. We could retire someplace for a spell until the heat passed, and things calmed down."

Jodi was thrilled to hear Jed include her in his plans, even if it did mean breaking the law. As he said, they were damned if they did, and damned if they didn't. So, it just didn't matter anymore.

CHAPTER 18

SAN ANTONIO TRUST

"THE BANK IS RIGHT IN THE HEART OF SAN ANTONIO, ON Military Plaza," Jodi said. "The whole square is covered in chili-con-carne stands where peasant women feed the city's workers lunch. Scores of people mill around and wait in line for their favorite chili. Before we rob the bank, we've got to try some. It's the best in Texas."

The female outlaw smiled like she was having a grand time. The planning sure did seem to come to her naturally. It was uncanny how Jodi saw things. Most people would try to break into the bank at night when it was closed. She said the best time would be during broad daylight because it would create a panic. They could sneak away amid the turmoil and confusion by simply mixing in the fleeing crowd.

She carefully planned it out. She made a diagram of the streets and the bank's layout. The day before the robbery, she went in to ask for change in her new white dress. The male clerk fell all over himself to please the beautiful woman. Meanwhile, Jodi checked out every exit and window. She watched where they got the money and noted the safe's door was standing partially open.

Banks had been the target of outlaws since the first one opened. They were broken into at night or on a weekend when the thieves had time to blow the safe. It could turn into a nightmare if they used dynamite, though. She believed it would be best to walk right through the front door and take all the money the teller had in his drawer and everything in the safe. When she was casing the place, she noticed white cloth sacks inside the vault. She believed they were full of money. Hopefully, they would still be there the next time she entered with a less friendly demeanor.

They rode into San Antonio from the south. There were so many people on the streets, they hardly stood out. They were just three more travelers passing through. You could tell the southern veterans who chose to flee to Texas. Their eyes were empty, and they wore remnants of Confederate clothing. The plaza was just beginning to fill with people. It would be noon in half an hour, and the plaza would be packed.

"Come on, boys," Jodi said and smiled like she was having the time of her life. Her counterparts warily looked for danger in every direction.

"My pa and I came here sometimes to buy things for the ranch. My daddy showed me the best chili-con-carne stand in the whole danged town," Jodi explained, just as excited about lunch as she was the bank heist. "As you can see, there are dozens of them."

Jed looked at Jodi like she was crazy. "You weren't kidding about eating before we rob the bank, were ya?" he whispered.

"Of course not." Jodi smiled. "What has one got to do with the other? I'm so hungry I could eat a horse. Come on, follow me." She grabbed Jed's wrist and added, "You'll be sorry if you miss out. I promise you won't regret it."

They sat down at a long table with benches along each side. The woman served the chili-con-carne in a ceramic bowl, and Jodi ordered two for each one of them. Once they had the first bite, they quickly devoured the chili and called for another bowl.

"What did I tell you? Finger lickin' good, right?" she stated with a big smile.

Jody grinned as she wiped her lips with the back of her hand, smudging her blood-red lipstick. Finally, when they finished, the plaza church bell began to ring. It was twelve noon.

Gong, gong, gong...rang the heavy bells.

Jed dropped some coins on the table, and the three got to their feet and turned toward the San Antonio First National Bank, located right on the plaza corner.

They were wearing their new clothes, and the men looked dapper beside the dark-haired beauty. Jed normally saw Jodi in nothing but denim britches. When he got a look at her in a dress, he could hardly pull his eyes away.

Jed still denied the feelings he already knew he had for the woman, though. For some dark reason, he continued to resist. Hell, even he didn't know why. She obviously had feelings for him, but he chose to ignore them just the same.

The beautiful woman struggled to keep a brilliant smile on her face, even if Jed didn't dote on her. She still had high hopes of getting her man. They looked like any three employees from some affluent business as they strolled through the plaza. The mix of customers was surprising. Men in suits, ties, and hats sat next to cowboys and laborers. Hardly anyone spoke as they devoured the delicious food, served by the poorest women in the city. Jodi, Jed, and John were just three more San Antonians getting a quick lunch before going back to work.

When they stepped up to the front of the bank, it was impressive. The building was almost as big as a church. It was evident the locals worshiped both money and God. Jodi grinned as she gave each of her partners a white hood with cut-out holes for their eyes. At the bottom, she even thought to sew in a drawstring to keep them tight, so the eyeholes didn't move, leaving them visually impaired. In a holdup, they wanted to see everything that happened.

They pulled the door closed, slipped the hoods over their heads and scanned the large lobby. Jodi immediately flipped the OPEN sign over, indicating the bank was CLOSED. Three tellers attended customers. It looked like a moderately busy day.

The bank teller Jodi talked to the day before smiled as he raised his eyes to see who was coming in. As soon as he saw the dark barrels of three large revolvers, his smile dissolved. Fear filled his eyes, and he glanced at his boss, who was sitting behind him.

Jodi raised her finger to her lips. Even with the mask, he understood the gesture. He stood frozen as Jed and John went over to the other tellers and pointed their revolvers in their faces.

"All you clients waiting in line, get on the floor right now, or I'll shoot ya where ya stand!" John shouted. "Facedown moron," he yelled at an obese man who lay on his back. "I wanna see noses touching the floor, ladies, and gentlemen, and I mean now! Any of you so much a look our way I'll shoot y'all to hell. Just one of you screw this up, and you'll all die."

The three outlaws knew it was an idle threat. John and Jed only shot Union soldiers, political leaders or government officials—not civilians. They figured those people calling the shots and giving the orders were just as responsible as the men in uniform. They had nothing against the bank customers and had no real intention of harming them unless things went sideways. If they did, as often occurred, then all bets were off.

"Put all the cash in the bag," Jed said as he produced a burlap sack. "If you move quickly, this will all be over before you know it, and nobody's gonna get hurt."

Jed nodded to John as he took over the two tellers, and Jed turned his attention to the man sitting shocked behind the highly polished desk. The nameplate said, Eli Walter Burns—Bank Manager.

"Hello, Mr. Burns," Jed said in a sweet southern drawl. "Would you be so kind as to help me get the money from the safe? I sure would appreciate your assistance. You do as we say, and I won't hurt a single little hair on that shiny bald head of yours."

Jed's eyes were haunting, and even with the mask on, the bank manager could see how hollow they were. He knew the man behind the mask was acquainted with violence and did as instructed. They each grabbed two white sacks. The bank director couldn't get his off the ground, so he dragged them across the floor and to the door.

"Now, you can join the rest of the folks on the floor, Mr. Burns," Jed said and patted him on the back. "You did well, sir. Your reward is your life. All of you kind folks keep your noses pinned to the floor for the next five minutes. One of us will stay behind and watch the door while the others run for the hills. If any of you get up or turn your head, you'll be shot dead. Everybody keep calm; it's almost over."

A man on the floor nervously removed his wallet and lay it beside him. Then another customer did the same. A woman pushed her purse away so they could have her money, too. All wanted to survive the robbery and live another day. It couldn't be over soon enough.

"I'm sorry. I didn't inform you folks that we're southern gentlemen," John said to the White men and women laying before him. "We don't steal from honest folks. We only rob banks that steal poor folks' land to sell it for large profits. Rest easy and keep your money.

"I apologize for the inconvenience. What we took from the bank will be insured. Nobody but the bank will lose a cent."

Under the mask, John's grin grew. The bank-robbing business might just work after all. He liked it.

The manager lifted his head to protest, but the click of a cylinder turning changed his mind. Nobody else moved as the three bank robbers pulled their masks from her faces and walked out into the massive crowd with five bags of money. It was odd they were carrying bags, but they were dressed as bankers themselves. Nobody paid them the slightest attention.

They walked over three blocks where they tied their horses. They lashed the sacks together, threw them over their saddles and walked the animals out of town. The city was so big there was no way they would get caught. They left San Antonio and rode directly for a spot Jodi found to hide the money.

After taking a reasonable amount of cash and stuffing it in their jackets, the three bank robbers hid their take under a distinguishable tree. They buried it deep under a sizable rock. It was a safe place to keep so much money.

They hadn't expected to get away with that much cash. They all were surprised there was twenty-two thousand dollars in the white cloth sacks, and they escaped without a scratch on them or the victims.

They dressed back into their traveling clothes and rode right back into town. They stopped again in another haberdashery on their way to the hotel and purchased new outfits. The clothes weren't formal but cast them as well-off ranch owners. From there, they proceeded to one of the best hotels in town.

They rented the best three rooms in the most exclusive hotel in the city. Who would look for the bank robbers right here San Antonio living it up in luxury? They had a fancy dinner in the hotel restaurant and a bottle of champagne. Neither John nor Jed had ever tried it, and the bubbles tickled their throats. It made their stomachs upset too.

As they walked through the massive hotel lobby, Jodi whispered, "I can't wait to see tomorrow's newspapers. We can read them at breakfast."

Jodi laughed so hard people looked her way. She had to sit down on a lobby couch. Still, nobody paid them much attention. San Antonio was a cow town, and many big ranchers frequented the hotel. Perhaps they were a little rough around the edges, but their money was just as good as the next man's.

"We need to buy ourselves a place to hide, since we've got the money. Any respectable outlaw gang has a hideout," Jodi explained. "But I thought, what better place to hide than in plain sight, right here in San Antonio. We could rob banks in the neighboring cities and live right here in town.

"As long as nobody knows who we are. I don't fancy living in some cave in the mountains. I like hiding in the city. With masks, nobody can identify us; one place is just as good as the other. I bet the newspaper even get it wrong."

They all were tired from the tension and excitement, not alone digging a six-foot-deep hole to hide the money. They were bushed. So, each headed for their respective rooms. Jed and John seemed happy to be in such a place and have the softest beads they'd ever felt.

The excitement of the day left all three bank robbers exhausted. In minutes they were fast asleep on the soft feather mattresses and pillows. None of them ever slept in such luxury.

The following day, Jed woke his partners bright and early and said, "Well, let's go down and have breakfast. They had a stack of newspapers there yesterday. Maybe we'll be in today's news!"

When they settled in at a fancy white table with cushioned bench seats on both sides, a waiter came straight over to take their order.

"Good morning, friends," the polite waiter said with a foreign accent. "What would you all like today?"

"How about we start with coffees for each while we think on it," Jed said. "And bring us a newspaper, please."

The waiter quickly returned with coffee in a large silver pot. He poured them each a cup and asked if they wished sugar, cream, or both. When he finished, he left the aromatic coffee pot in the middle of the table while he disappeared to find the newspaper.

He was back in less than a minute, handed Jed the periodical and left. Jed looked down at the paper and then back up to Jodi and John. He was almost afraid to open it. What if somehow, they figured out who they were. Sure, Jed was a sniper and had shot countless enemies. But he never in his wildest dreams thought he would rob a bank.

Jodi snatched the paper away. Her impatience with men was more than she could bear. She opened it to the front page, and the headlines said, *OUTLAW GANG STEALS $50,000 FROM THE FIRST NATIONAL BANK IN MILITARY PLAZA.*

Jodi continued to read bits of the article and then proclaimed: "Here it says three Black men did it. It says we were probably desperate slaves. I guess they noticed your voice, John. Jed's heavy southern accent might have made them think he was Black, too. I must say our luck is holding fine. Since I didn't talk, they'll never imagine a White woman was with the gang. How do you boys like that for planning?"

"We didn't steal no fifty thousand dollars," John said.

Jed smiled and replied, "The banks be the biggest thieves of them all. We rob them for twenty-two thousand, and they claim fifty thousand from the insurance company. Who are the outlaws now?"

CHAPTER 19

SPARK & COURT

THEY ALL SPENT THEIR DAY VISITING PLACES THEY COULD never afford before. The newfound fortune let them dine in the best restaurants and shop the best shops. John had only been shopping for himself since he rode with Jed. He was like a child in a candy store.

The general store was one of the places he made a beeline for. He looked at all the glass jars full of candy canes, lollipops, jawbreakers, and chocolate bonbons. He ordered three of each. The woman behind the counter filled three small paper bags, and the trio strolled through town eating the sweet morsels and being fascinated by the city.

They used the whole day to shop, eat and sightsee. It was a first for the two war-torn men, and Jodi used her knowledge to take them on a grand tour. Her father's ranch made good profits at one time, which allowed them to occasionally visit the places she took Jed and John. Finally, after dinner, the men were all walked out, although Jodi was still willing to go on late into the night. Jed and John had developed sleeping patterns over the years, and it was time for them to go to bed. They bid each other good night and retired for the evening.

Each room had a door attached to the next, so if trouble arrived unexpectedly, they could advise each other and flee. The outlaws always kept their travel kits ready and beside the window just in case.

Late that night, Jed suddenly awoke. At first, he thought danger was the culprit and reached under his pillow for his revolver. Then he heard crying coming from the next room. He knew it was Jodi, but he couldn't quite figure out why she was upset. She seemed so happy with how the bank robbery worked out. She seemed to be exhilarated by the whole thing. Still, there was little doubt the sobbing came from the room next to Jed's.

At first, he walked over and held his ear to the adjoining door. He wasn't mistaken. He could tell she was trying to muffle her sobs, but they passed through the thin walls and made Jed's heart ache. He didn't know why hearing her cry disturbed him so much, but he tapped lightly on the door anyway. There was no answer. He knocked again, this time with his knuckles. The sobs and crying became more muffled, like Jodi was holding her hand over her mouth so he wouldn't hear her.

Women. What in the world can be wrong now?

As silently as he could, he pushed her door open, although only a crack to make sure she was presentable. He didn't want her to think he was stalking her or had ill intentions.

"Jodi?" Jed whispered just a little louder and crept forward toward her bed.

Her heart raced and jumped to her throat. Jodi's voice changed in an instant. "Yes?" she asked and grabbed for Jed's wrist. When she spoke, she didn't open her eyes.

"I can't hide it any longer," she said as more tears ran down her cheeks.

She lay back again, embarrassed. When she opened her eyes, Jodi tried to blink the tears away and closed them again. Jed leaned down to console her, his hand caressing her soft cheek. She would do anything to get Jed close enough to steal a kiss, and he would do anything to stop her from crying. He was so close she felt his hot breath on her neck.

Her blue eyes sparkled when she opened them again and her red lips smiled. Her heart pitter-pattered and her breath became hot and short.

His lips were inches from hers. She sighed deeply and leaned into Jed. The emotions swirled as their lips met.

She could feel his heart hammer in his chest. They were both charged with electricity. Invisible bolts of lightning shot between the would-be lovers.

Jed wrapped his arms around her and held her tight. She felt like she had been waiting for his embrace her whole life. The rest of the night was like a magic dream, the kind that left you wondering what really happened when you finally awakened.

Passion overflowed as she pulled him next to her in the luxurious bed. Their hands pulled at their scant clothing as their lips hungrily tangled in desire. Finally, Jodi straddled Jed, her knees slightly bent and her hands gripping the headboard. Nature took its course. Their passion unleased, the two young people moved in unison, waltzing to a lover's tune filled with emotion.

Deeply satisfied, sleep came slowly to Jodi. Her skin tingled all over as she spooned her lover. His breathing was slow and even and, every so often, a snore escaped. She carefully grabbed his wrist and wrapped his arm around her. She curled up with his hand snuggled to her chin. Only then could she sleep, and it was instant. She was tired and satisfied. She had longed for Jed for weeks. Now, she wished the night would never end.

"Hey, there, sunshine," Jed said the following morning when she opened her eyes. She rubbed the sleep away with the balls of her fists and pulled the covers tight up to her chin.

"I'm cold," Jodi complained. "Come back...please."

"We've both got to the get up right now, darlin'," Jed said. "John will be waiting on us."

She was startled for a moment. It was the first time Jed called her an endearment. Should she dare wish last night wasn't a one-night stand? Men were like that. As bad as the situation was, she knew better. Their life together wasn't going to be like the fairy tales she read. He was no prince in shining armor. He was an outlaw, and now she was, too. There would be nobody coming to rescue them, she was sure. She knew the law and the Army both would give chase. It was the hand life dealt them, so they had to play it as best they could.

Sure, she was almost as much an outlaw as Jed and John. They all were the products of a series of circumstances and of no choice in the path they chose. Shit happened no matter how well you planned or how honest you were.

JOHN LAY awake in his bed in the fancy hotel they chose to stay in for a night or two. They planned to buy three extra horses, bullets, and dynamite tomorrow. You just never knew when it might come in handy. They figured the wolves would be held at bay until they could figure out where they would go next.

For some reason, he couldn't sleep a wink. Maybe it was all the excitement. He wasn't getting any younger. He figured he must be around fifty, but he wasn't sure. It didn't say on the ownership papers. At least, that was what Master Noland told him. Black folks weren't allowed to learn to read and write on the plantation.

He was a cruel owner but wiser than John had known at the time. If you educate ignorant men, you create competitors. Naïve and smart were two different things. A genius without any education is just another fool. Educated slaves was the last thing pro-slavery Southerners wanted. With the war over; many ex-slaves wandered foolishly without direction.

Now, he hoped young Black boys and girls would finally be given the opportunity to at least receive an education. He imagined more freedom would come with time. Time, however, was quickly disappearing for him. Nonetheless, he wanted to enjoy at least some of the life he had left. Life as a slave was void of enjoyment, especially during the war. The war was indeed hell. Even though they were on the run, it was the best he'd lived for as long as John could remember.

He looked back on the last years of his life. For many, things had gotten worse. Life had been pretty much the same for him, but now it was better. He and his friend lived through more conflicts than he could recall. So far, they've managed to escape with their lives and all of their limbs. He reckoned he was a fortunate man, even if they were on the run. He'd been running from something his whole life anyway. At least now, he wasn't alone.

Who knows? Maybe one day, they would find a place where they could live like ordinary folks, enjoying peace without having to look over their shoulders.

They certainly had enough money. Who would have expected them to walk into a bank right in the middle of the city and rob it? It was almost too easy. At last, he was amazed. He laid in the softest bed he'd ever slept in, and he couldn't sleep a wink. Maybe he was excited to see what was in store for the three of them in the future.

He wondered if he would remember how to act like a civilized man after all they'd seen and done. Hell, he was never allowed to choose a side to fight for. Of course, he would have chosen the Union, given a choice. It was a secret he would carry to his grave.

He just didn't know how Jed would take it, him being a full-blooded Southerner and all. That didn't mean he approved of slavery, though. He was what people called a *southern gentleman*. There were few of such men left nowadays.

Quantrill's marauders were a strange and foreboding mix of men. Some of them were the evilest men he'd ever known—men like Bloody Bill Anderson and Jesse James. Others, like Jed and he, were good men sent out to do the devil's work. The last years had been a human calamity. Now, they were going to try to enjoy life, however long or short it was to be. Every outlaw knew, in the end, they all got caught or killed. Or did they? Maybe, just maybe, they would be the exception to the rule, Noland fantasized.

CHAPTER 20

THE OLD GANG

WHEN FRANK AND JESSE JAMES WALKED INTO THE SALOON in San Antonio, Jed and John's hearts nearly stopped. Had one of the captain's followers sent the James brothers to hunt them down? What else would bring them to Texas? They all wintered here during the war, but it wasn't winter, and the war was over. Jesse was deeply involved in Missouri and Kansas politics, and Jed doubted he would abandon his state without reason. Maybe he, too, was on the run.

Jed and John gripped the handles of their pistols below the table. All the while, their faces were as though chiseled from stone. Not a hint of an expression showed on either man. Jodi looked at the two men at the door and back to Jed and John. She was puzzled. She knew better than saying anything, though. They had that threatening look in their eyes.

The strangers made a quick glance across the room. They deemed it safe and walked to the bar. Apparently, they didn't recognize Jed and John in their fancy new duds. The James brothers were well dressed, too. Both

Jed and John would know those faces anyplace, especially Jesse. His eyes were unforgettable. They'd known the brothers for years and fought alongside Frank.

"What's going on with you two?" Jodi grumbled, unable to refrain from asking.

They acted like she wasn't even there. She noticed both men's gun hands were under the table, and their eyes were boring holes in the men who entered. One looked to be quite a bit younger than the other. Jodi's heart stopped for just a second when she looked in those wild eyes. It was like looking at a savage animal. Instinctively, she suspected the men had been sent to kill Jed and John.

The tension in the Millbury Saloon rose. The presence of the men at the bar created the most commotion. Nobody knew who they were, but they all smelled trouble. Every man at every table tried not to look their way. Jesse leaned his back against the bar, propping himself up with his elbows. His eyes moved slowly across the patrons. Most men stared at their cards or down at their table. Some glared into their glasses and swirled the liquid. The only person who refused to avoid eye contact with the stranger at the bar was Jodi. Jesse noticed straight away. He had always been alert that way. Frank had his back to the tables, ignoring the antics of his brother and sipped at his whiskey.

First, Jesse winked at Jodi, making her blush. That was when he noticed both John and Jed. The Black scout, he couldn't miss from a half mile away. Jed cut off years of hair and beard, but Jesse remembered those eyes, too. They were like his when he looked in the mirror.

He elbowed his brother and grinned, then nodded his head toward the table where the bank robbers sat. As Jesse smiled at the three, Frank remained impossible to read. He wasn't as dangerous as Jesse, though, and seldom acted irrationally. His brother was so impulsive, many suspected one day it would lead to his demise.

"Well, well, well, if it ain't the captain's old sniper team," Jesse James said just loud enough for the three of them to hear. He waltzed to their table like he was the town mayor.

"Ain't ya gonna invite two old friends to sit down?" he asked.

"Old friends don't need an invite, Jesse." Jed smiled. "Grab a chair and fill your glasses, boys. Howdy Frank. How you been?"

"We come down here to round up some of the boys to start a gang," Jesse said as he huddled with the four. He didn't beat around the bush and knew he could confide in both Jed and John.

"Are you boys interested in signing up with us?" Jesse continued. As if an afterthought, Jesse looked at Jodi he added, "Excuse my poor manners, ma'am. This is my brother Frank James, and I'm Jesse. Maybe my old pards told you about us."

"Excuse me. I forgot my manners," Jed said. "This is Jodi Goodnight."

Jodi smiled at Jesse James as boldly as anyone dared. She wasn't impressed with all the newspaper articles and his sass. She held her ground and told him what she thought.

"We have a gang," she said, making Jesse laugh. Then she whispered, "Did you hear about the bank robbery right here in downtown San Antonio yesterday? That was us."

"Nah, that can't be true. Is it Jed?" Frank asked, genuinely surprised. "I didn't take you two for that type. Maybe you ought to join up with us. All of us who rode with Quantrill are hunted by the Army anyway. We ain't got a damned thing to lose."

Jed pulled a newspaper from his back pocket and tossed it on the saloon table. Frank unfolded the paper and flattened the article with his hand, then held it up to the dim kerosine lamp. He read the entire article as Jesse tried to grab the paper from his hands.

"Hold your horses, Jesse," Frank ordered. "How did you two pull this off?"

"It wasn't our idea," John said. "It was Jodi who thought the whole thing up. You know we've never done much more than shoot folks from afar throughout the entire war. Even I find myself surprised when I realize I'm a bank robber. But if it weren't for Miss Goodnight here, we'd still be stealing food off windowsills and shirts off clotheslines."

"You're joshing, right?" Jesse asked, finding it hard to believe a woman could devise such a plan. "Are you kin to Goodnight, the rancher?"

"He's my uncle. Maybe y'all want to join our outlaw gang?" Jodi asked, more in jest than anything.

Jesse took it as a challenge, though. He was an alfa male and never liked being outshined, no matter the situation and especially by a woman.

"Me? I don't follow the orders of a woman," Jesse said incredulously. "I don't fancy that at all, no offense, Miss Jodi. You sure could have fooled me. And here y'all sit in the middle of San Antonio right after you robbed the bank. Y'all have got balls, I'll give ya that—excuse my French."

"Did you boys hear Captain Quantrill was shot and killed in Kentucky by Union soldiers?" Frank asked. "As soon as Jesse and I took off, we already knew they'd be after us. When I heard the news, we gave up the cause.

Oh, we're gonna wreak the wrath on the Yankees in Kansas and Missouri but by robbing their banks. That's how you hurt a Yankee the most. Strike at his pocket."

"I want to be the first outlaw to rob a train," Jesse bragged. "They forced us into this life, so we might as well reap the rewards. If not, we fought for four years for diddly squat. I haven't quite figured it out yet, but I'm going to find a way. We need a few more men first, though."

"What happened to the Youngers?" John asked. "The brothers could make good partners for you, and three or four of them will probably be willin' to run with ya. The Army will be after them just like the rest of us."

"So, you two ain't interested?" Frank asked. "The money would be worth your while."

"We've already got more money than I've ever seen. I wouldn't mind passing a spell spending some of it," John replied, smiling. "To be honest, we thought you boys were coming down here to find us and take us back to what's left of the Raiders."

"We lit out right after you two did," Jesse said. "There ain't much left of the boys, and Union army be running all over the countryside looking for us. We plan to keep 'em busy, though. I doubt they even remember who you two are anymore, what with all that's happened. With the captain dead, maybe they'll let up some."

"Our names are on the rosters, and the Yankees probably got them all. Payroll records will work the same. They'll know who we are. Whether they can find us or not is another thing," Jed said.

Jesse James couldn't sit still. He'd sit and talk for a spell; then he'd get up and pace the floor. His fingers played compulsively over the leather of his holster, where his Colt revolver rested. He appeared more like a tiger in a cage than a young man. He was eager for action; that much was clear.

"I heard Cole Younger was down this way," Jesse said. "Who knows, he may be in San Antonio, too. It has the best red-light district in all of Texas. Excuse the reference, ma'am." The young outlaw tipped his hat out of respect.

All four had one thing in common—they acted like relative gentlemen in the presence of a woman. Jodi couldn't help but like them, even though she knew the James brothers were killers. Frank seemed almost gentle, and Jesse was just another lost soul who was all mixed up from the conflict. He bore mental wounds that would never heal.

"If we run into any of the Youngers, we'll let 'em know you're lookin' for 'em," John said. "Hopefully, you'll be as lucky as us."

"Oh, I ain't lookin' to rob one bank or train," Jesse said as his grin grew. His eyes got that crazy look again. "I intend to rob a dozen of each until I bankrupt one or the other. I'm gonna steal their money until they ain't got no more."

"Until one day they catch us," Frank said.

"Bullshit," Jesse spat. "There ain't a soldier alive that can outdraw or outshoot me. Not from the North or South. Ain't that right, boys? Well, maybe except for Jed here with a long rifle."

Jesse was so full of spirit Jodi couldn't stop smiling. Even the most outlandish things he said seemed possible. She knew he was a cold-blooded killer, but half the men in the country were after the war. Some were just more deadly than others.

CHAPTER 21

HOSTILES

IN THE DISTANCE THEY SAW VULTURES MAKING LAZY circles in the sky, beyond a stand of trees. Not just two or three, but dozens. When the bank robbers neared the carnage, many more predators took flight. As they got closer, they saw four-legged scavengers attacking bloated bodies. There were so many flies, Jodi had to wag her hand before her face to shoo them away. The buzzing could be heard from a fair distance.

Jodi already was anxious—actually, she was a little crazed. They used their bandanas to stifle the wretched stench as they approached the massacre. Bodies covered the ground. Men in blue uniforms lay dead from arrows, spears, and gunshot wounds.

It was nothing new to Jed and John. They'd seen countless killing fields during the war. It was Jodi's first experience to see what men could do to each other. It was sobering.

"This looks like it may have been another one of those patrols looking for us," John said, emotionless. "If they were tracking Comanche, they'd be in greater numbers. I reckon this be the second lot of men sent from Kansas to kill us. The Comanche did us a favor."

Jed reached down and picked up a torn and tattered flier. He got a bad taste in his mouth when he looked at it. He passed it to John, but they didn't show it to Jodi. John folded up the wanted poster and slipped it into his shirt pocket.

Jodi was in such shock she didn't even notice. She hadn't seen their faces with the reward printed on the piece of Union paper.

"When you pray for rain, you gotta deal with the mud," Jodi said, her voice cracked as she looked around with a furrowed brow. "Where you find one Comanche, usually there be a twenty or more."

"We need to leave all this dreary shit behind," Jed spat. "I'm tired of running from just about everybody we run into."

"Then we don't run," John said decidedly. "We know something they don't. You can shoot the ears off a Comanche at five hundred yards. I figure if we lay in wait and ambush 'em, we can take out enough of the rascals they turn and go home."

"Indians don't like to lose too many warriors in a battle," Jodi added from experience with hostiles back at her family's ranch. "It makes too many wives unhappy back in the village. If we do a good enough job, they'll know better than to mess with us again. Most war parties look for easy targets."

"What if they don't come back?" Jed asked.

"Then we'll have to go find them before they find us," John said. "I can hunt Indians, too. They be a mite trickier than Yankees, but if they're not ghosts, I can track 'em."

Again, they found an excellent spot to shoot from

with the sun at their backs. They set up in a position higher than the valley and with plenty of rock cover. It was hot again, and Jed and John were covered in twigs and branches as they lay with the spyglass and rifle scope pointed into the distance. They knew the Indians would return to have a second look at what they could take from the soldiers. The dead soldiers still wore their boots and coats. So, it was probably only a matter of time.

"It appears they won the fight, took the important valuables—horses, guns, gold, and silver—and rode back to their camp," Jodi said. "You just watch. After a while, they'll decide they probably left some valuables. They'll come back for a second peek when things are quieter. I reckon they grabbed what they could and ran for the hills. The gunshots could be heard for miles, but it looks like there wasn't anybody to hear 'em. The Comanche didn't know that, though. They'll do another grab-and-run for sure. Once it's dark, they'll come crawlin' back this way."

Jodi had a hell of a lot more experience with the Comanche than Jed and John. The hostiles steered clear of the warring combatants of the Civil War. Their numbers and weaponry were too great.

The men hoped Jodi was right. Many of the Indians targeted the smaller ranches and farms for livestock, horses and just about anything else they could steal. The people populated their land, so they took anything they found on their property. It was the law of the land. Only the White men didn't see things that way.

Jed rubbed his hands up and down his face trying to keep sharp. They had waited all day, and it would soon be dark. The moon would come up about an hour or so after nightfall, which would probably be when the

Comanche returned. They would take advantage of the darkness. That left a small window for the hostiles to get everything of value. Jed would have to shoot by starlight. Lucky for him, there wasn't a cloud in the sky.

Soon the sun set just above the western mountains. It appeared to grow, magnified by the humidity, before it disappeared. It left behind a curtain of darkness. Just before the light failed, Jed pulled his bandana off and wrapped it over his eyes, and his vision dove into darkness. He wanted his eyes to adjust to no light at all so his vision would be enhanced when it came time to look down the rifle scope at the target. Hopefully, he would be able to pick out silhouettes as they neared the dead scattered across the field.

John scanned the bodies with his spyglass. He swept the glass across the diminished field of vision. The braver animals began feeding on the dead again. Others waited, knowing humans were nearby. They patiently sat at the edge of the tree line.

"They must have taken their wounded and dead when they initially finished the battle," Jodi whispered. "They be like that with their people."

Not a single Comanche was seen dead, but earlier, John noted bloodstains and pieces of bodies where no corpse lay. The battle appeared vicious, so men had to have died on both sides. Even though the remaining bodies were all Yankees, they felt bad for them just the same.

Hell, the war was over. When would the killing stop? There was so much hate. America was split in two. The North hated the South, and the South detested the North. Of course, everybody loathed the Indians and the Mexicans. Where would it stop? In the past, they cursed the Spanish and the English, too. The cycle never ended.

Just like expected, dark images hovered over the bodies as one Comanche and then another crept out onto the killing field. It was as though they sensed the danger; but their greed for what they left overpowered their normal caution. John lay his hand on the shooter's shoulder. It was the signal for Jed to get ready. The killing field was repopulated with another ten Comanche braves. They went through the dead men's clothing, pulling off their boots and coats. Some removed shiny metal buttons.

Jodi had stashed the horses a mile away in a deep gorge where they couldn't be seen. Three animals were easy to hide. These Indians already had all the horses they wanted. They had the Army mounts from the morning battle.

One of the warriors stopped his search and instinctively looked toward the people hiding in the blind. He moved his hand to his knife and walked over bodies as he came closer. Jodi was on Jed's left side and John on his right. When Jodi looked with her eyes spread wide, John had vanished. He'd disappeared without a word. Panic began to eat at the cowgirl's nerves. These weren't just outlaws; they were Comanche, every White woman's nightmare.

The single Comanche continued to approach their position. It was almost like he sensed their presence. Suddenly, though, there was a blur of motion, and an excruciating pain ravaged the warriors' ribs. The Comanche gasped for breath but couldn't seem to get his lungs to work. The pain, like a giant fiery ball, exploded up and down his ribcage. Then a second rifle butt hit his head and his pain subsided. He fell unconscious. Gray matter seeped from the crack in his skull.

Just as quickly as he disappeared, John was back

beside Jed and Jodi. He tapped the shooter on the shoulder, and Jed pulled off his blindfold, only opening one eye. He immediately saw several dark images hovering over the White men's bodies. The first report was so loud it made Jodi's ears ring. She never heard the second and third.

As soon as Jed made the next shot, he reloaded the Sharps rifle. In not much more than a second, he was aiming again. John tapped him on the shoulder all through the sniper attack. They worked as if they had developed some sort of unheard code that allowed them to eliminate their enemies without speaking. The Indians knew where the bullets came from by the barrel flashes, but their gunfire couldn't penetrate the rock cover John selected.

To Jodi, it seemed like an hour of deafening rifle blasts, especially when the Comanche tried to approach their position. John opened fire with his Henry rifle. They'd never know for sure, but few Comanche escaped that night. The sniper team made short work of the rest of the aggressors.

They waited until the moon rose. It looked like a giant orange as it cast a tinted glow across their faces. Before Jodi knew it, both Jed and John disappeared. She knew they were checking to make sure all the enemy was dead, though. It was ironic how now Jed and John would end up with the silver and gold taken from the same soldiers who hunted ex-Raiders.

As Jed and John crawled through the enemy bodies, they checked each brave. Several had pouches of gold and silver they stole the morning before from the many who lay dead beside them. They confiscated all the extra bullets they carried, and there were a lot. By the time they returned, they had two sacks full.

Again, her eyes were spread so wide; only the whites sparkled in the dark. Each time they left, she couldn't help but think Comanche surrounded her. She would rather face a dozen Union soldiers than one Comanche. That was how bad they terrorized her during her youth. She still had nightmares about being captured and stolen from her father. Even after he died, they continued. In her dreams, though, her father was still alive but couldn't reach her to rescue her from a woman's worst nightmare.

"Ya wanna point that thing in a different direction?" Jed asked, smiling kindly. "All the bad folks after us are dead. At least for the time being."

"Maybe we can travel and enjoy ourselves for a spell," John said, and he was smiling too.

"I'll feel better when we get away from this place," Jodi said. "You called it a killing field. That sounds appropriate. Let's go."

They felt their way across the landscape beneath a moon that lengthened three shadows. They carefully led their horses until they arrived at the main road. Once there, they mounted and rode off into the night.

CHAPTER 22

MEXICO

Jodi sat hunched over a set of bank plans she had spread across a table. This got a microscopic grin from Jed. He studied her for another second before he sat down beside her. They found a small town in Mexico where Yankee soldiers were not welcome. Sure, the Apache and Comanche still roamed the region, but word got out about Jed's skills. They even gave him a name—something that surprised them all. They heard it from two Indian scouts they met outside of the small Mexican village. They told them they had information of interest but wouldn't divulge the secret until they paid them for their gossip.

"The Comanche call you, *He who sees in the dark*," Potak, the Tonkawa medicine man, said.

"That's an awfully long name, ain't it?" Jed asked.

"What is your White man's name?" his cousin Tuc asked. When Jed looked into the warrior's eyes, he got a bad feeling. It was like a shadow just floated over his soul.

"Jed," he replied.

"That's not a name." Potak laughed. "That's a sound, much like a fart. *He who sees in the dark* is a much better name. It was well worth the dollar, wasn't it?"

Despite the comment, they all laughed.

"It's pretty hard to get a shorter name than Jed unless it's Ed," John said. "Even I got a longer name than that."

"What's your full name then?" Jed asked, curious. He peeked at Jodi from the corner of his eyes. Her skin was dark from the sun, the color of olives. Her black hair hung down her back. While they were in town, she took to wearing a dress most days. Only on the days, they went out for a ride did she change back into her denim britches and flannel shirt.

"John Washington Noland." He smiled. "Actually, my name is John Washington now and nothing more from today onward. I ain't gonna keep the name of the man who owned me and sent me off to fight and die in his name. He was a coward for not going himself and a bastard for not giving me my freedom. That's a man I would not mind meeting again."

"That's a fine name, John," Jodi said. "Washington, just like our first president."

Later they all sat on a cantina porch. Jed had his chair leaned up against the wall and was puffing on a cheroot as John made up a hand-built cigarette. He licked the paper, wrapped it tight, and dipped the end in his mouth before turning it around and popping it between his lips. He scratched a match to life on the porch post and fired it up. Jodi sat on the edge with her legs dangling. She was kicking them back and forth and savoring a candy cane. There was a comfortable silence between them. They were finally safe and relaxed.

"You know, I've been over the plans, and we can rob the second bank in less than ten minutes if we work together," Jodi said. "I was thinking about the bank we robbed in San Antonio and picked out the places where we wasted time."

"Why so much rush?" John asked.

"To keep from getting caught by the sheriff," Jodi replied. "I figure with every minute we're inside the bank our safety decreases and our chance of getting caught increases. If we are only there for five minutes, it hardly gives anybody time to run down to the sheriff and back again. We'd already be gone. We have to make this like a science."

"Whatcha talking about a science?" Jed laughed. "We're robbin' banks not inventing electricity."

"You're wrong, Jed," Jodi emphasized with a hard stare. Something gave him the feeling she was a bit peeved with him, but he couldn't figure out why. "Practically everything comes from science. So why not use science to rob banks when fools like Frank and Jesse James go in shooting up the place and hurting innocent people."

"All right, you've got my attention," Jed said and smiled patiently.

John Washington was already all ears. The first robbery went so well, and Jodi planned it all independently. It only made sense she could make it happen again and even better. He smiled for a moment. The war was truly over. Robbing banks without shooting the general population all to hell seemed a damned sight better than fighting your brothers and friends for some damned cause or other. Yeah, he could live with being a bank robber, he supposed. Shooting people for a living was a thing of the past. Well, at least until the Union army decided to collect on the bounties they saw in the killing field.

The cantina was near the edge of the little Mexican village, and the sunset was visible from the porch. Each one had a ringside seat for the spectacle they were about to witness. They passed around a bottle of tequila, and each poured two fingers into a glass. They sipped the harsh spirits as they enjoyed the view. A flock of geese flew in their habitual formation as rafts of clouds floated across the sky. Shades of pink streaked the heavens as the sun neared the horizon.

As the red ball of fire began to fall off the far side of the world, a battle of colors erupted in the distance. A prism of warriors surrendered to nightfall. Stars began to sparkle from the east and slowly stretched to the west, as the light began to vanish. They turned their faces skyward as the last warm rays rolled over their skin. Long wispy clouds glowed red, making the whole eastern horizon look like the world was on fire.

John contemplated the sunset. He took a last puff on his cigarette and flicked the butt into the street. He pulled out three cinnamon sticks and passed one to Jed and another to Jodi. As he sucked on the rock candy, John bathed in his newfound freedom.

Jed walked across the porch and sat down next to Jodi. She grabbed his arm and rested her head on his shoulder. She sighed.

"What's it like in Austin?" Jed asked.

Suddenly Jodi beamed, and her eyes twinkled mischievously. She began to tell them all the exciting places to visit and eat in the city. Many of them surrounded the Austin Central Bank.

CHAPTER 23

AUSTIN CITY BANK

THE STREETS IN DOWNTOWN AUSTIN WERE FULL OF locals and visitors. It was July 3, the day before the big holiday when many of the country folks came to town to escape the boredom of their daily struggle to survive. The Fourth of July promised a parade and fireworks to celebrate the nation's birth. Every merchant in the city was open, hoping to spike their sales with the vast array of visitors. Even the shoeshine boys had lines of men seeking a good polish and spit-shine.

On the boardwalks strolled groups of finely dressed ladies. Some carried parasols to protect their delicate skin from the harsh Texas sun. Salesmen of every description were present. From those who sold bars of lucky soap to fortune-tellers. Fraudulent doctors sold elixirs of alcohol and opium they said would cure everything and anything. Conmen operated shell games with the help of sholes, who claimed they had won to attract more suckers.

Inside a diner, sitting across from the bank, sat two men and a woman. All three appeared to be ready for mass. The woman carried what appeared to be two Bibles. One was the Old Testament and the other the New Testament. When the waiter delivered their meal, the lady led them in grace as she clutched one of the books to her chest. The room was full of affluent people. All the waiters and waitresses wore white uniforms.

The three sat before a large picture window in the front of the restaurant. It gave a perfect view of the street and beyond. Jed kept his eyes on the bank's front entrance. He closed his eyes for a moment as he studied the interior plan he memorized. Jodi worked out every detail, down to where they would eat.

They enjoyed iced tea with their meal. Jed watched as the crowds of people began to snake their way up and down the street. There was a carnival in town to reap the rewards of the large concentration of people. Inside was peaceful and quiet while they were getting ready for the party on the street.

The fine-dining restaurant was full for lunch. Everybody was in a good mood and preparing for the celebrations. When John pulled at his clerical collar, Jed's face got as red as a tomato. Jodi modestly pulled her stiff, white scarf tight over her head and tied it under her chin.

It wasn't unusual for a nun to accompany the local clergy as they ate with little conversation. They wore long black robes. Somewhere in the restaurant, a clock began to ring the time—twelve chimes. Jodi looked from Jed to John. They left money on the table for the bill and made their way toward the exit and the main street.

Wagons and horsemen passing on the street stopped to let the righteous trio cross the road unimpeded. The driver of a stopped buckboard wagon tipped his hat and made the sign of the cross, kissing his thumb and forefinger. The two priests returned the gesture and nodded knowingly as they slowly made their way to the opposite boardwalk. The door to the bank was open. It was nearly empty. Everybody was on the street watching all the excitement. The teller stood on his tiptoes to see the spectacle taking place outside the window.

Jodi watched the distracted man and turned the OPEN sign over to CLOSED. Jed and John shut the double doors behind them. The guard at the door looked puzzled but still didn't suspect anything unusual from two priests and a nun.

Jodi smiled at the man and bowed her head as she passed a Bible to each priest.

Jed and John opened the hollowed-out books and pulled out Colt revolvers. Before they knew what was happening, the lone teller and single guard were looking down the dark barrels of large pistols. Both quickly realized the men behind the pistols were not clergymen. Hammers were pulled back, and chambers clicked. That was enough for both bank men to raise their hands. Jodi looked back toward the safe, and just like she had seen the day before, it was slightly ajar, although she had no idea what was inside.

Jodi glanced at the stopwatch she bought for the robbery. She wanted to shave time off their jobs, if only by minutes or even seconds. She believed every extra second they were in the bank they became more vulnerable. John and Jed added their expertise from riding with Quantrill's Raiders and applied it to three different escape routes. In case one wasn't viable, they had alternatives. They also had extra clothing hidden and changes of horses stashed close enough for them to be changed and look like other people in thirty minutes from the moment they walked out of the bank.

Luckily, they brought the white bags from their first robbery in San Antonio as this time there were none. When Jed and Jodi walked into the vault, they almost fainted. Stacks of greenbacks filled a pallet. On the other side of the room was a pile of gold bricks.

"We'll need a buckboard wagon to get all this out of here," Jed said as he gawked at the mountain of bills.

"There's no way we can take it all," Jodi said. "It'll take too much time. Let's go; we've only got five minutes left."

"Whatcha mean five minutes?" John retorted. "If we make two trips, we can take twice as much. The horses are only three blocks away. Nobody's been to the door since we walked in. With the closed sign, they'll just think the bank shut up early because of the festivities."

"I agree with John," Jed said. "I've never imagined so much Yankee money in one place. I think we should take as much as we can. Hell, we're alone in here. We just have to figure how to get it out."

"You two fools do whatever you want," Jodi grumbled as she stuffed two white bags full of large denomination bills wrapped and bound in stacks of one hundred.

"Four minutes," Jodi declared.

When Jodi dragged the bags full of money to the front door, she removed her scarf and dropped the black robe to the floor. Underneath was her riding clothing. The gown was long enough even to cover her boots. She looked out the window.

"Times up, boys," she whispered. "Don't linger. I'm gone."

Then she pulled the door open and slipped out. Jodi struggled to the corner with the heavy sacks of money. There was a boy there shining shoes.

"You want to make a double eagle coin, young man?" she asked the teen and smiled her best smile.

He grabbed his hat from his head and replied, "Why sure, ma'am. What do I have to do?"

"Carry one of these sacks for me to my horse." Jodi smiled calmly. She appeared to be on a Sunday stroll.

"Why, for twenty dollars, I'll carry 'em both. I'm stronger than I look. I'm almost thirteen."

Jodi walked to the horses slowly as the boy labored under the heavy weight. Once they arrived where she left Sandy, she had him tie them together and throw them over the saddle.

Jodi messed his hair and smiled. She grabbed his chin and pulled a double eagle out of the pocket of her britches. She placed it in his hand, and he grinned.

His eyes lit up and he said, "Thank you ever so much, ma'am. I'm gonna go buy some rock candy."

"There's no need to tell anybody where you got the money, young man," Jodi warned. "You do want to be a gentleman, don't you?"

"Yes, ma'am. I sure do."

"What's your name?"

"Sammy...er, I mean Sam." he beamed, hoping to act older than he was.

"My name is Josephina," she said, "and this is a secret between a woman and a young man. Do you understand, Sam?"

"Yes, Miss Josephina," Sam replied and turned and ran off.

Jodi chuckled, then looked over at Jed and John's horses. They should have been here by now. She prayed they would not delay. She had it in her head that it was impossible to be caught if you spent less time vulnerable. Then again, there was a hell of a lot of money back there in the bank. She stepped up onto Sandy, turned her toward an alleyway and rode out of town. She would wait for the boys to arrive at the meeting spot.

It suddenly dawned on her exactly how much cash there was; she didn't even know how to begin to count it. Her sacks were mostly large bills and were already wrapped and stamped.

~

JED AND JOHN stuffed everything they could find full of money. Then they looked over at the gold.

"If we get everything here, we're never gonna have to commit another crime against society or the Almighty again," John said as he grinned from ear to ear. "How much money you reckon there be here, Jed. You're good with numbers."

Jed looked dumbfounded and replied, "I figure there be neigh on a million dollars. I reckon we're rich."

They already were counting their money when their bubble suddenly burst. There was a knock on the door. John and Jed still wore their priest's attire. Their traveling clothes were under their robes.

They looked at each other and frowned. They moved toward the door until they saw the man rap on the window again. He was using the end of a gun barrel, and he wore a tin star on his chest.

"I know y'all's in there," the marshal yelled out. "I've been watching you for neigh on five minutes. Now, open the damned door before I have to shoot the glass out."

He had a large revolver in his hand, and it was pointing right at John and Jed. They looked over at their pistols on the director's desk. They laid them down when they began to collect the cash. It had only been fifteen minutes since Jodi left, but it looked like they stayed a few minutes too long, just as Jodi had said.

Their guns were so close, yet so far away. If they moved for them, the marshal would gun them down. They didn't stand a chance.

As Jed raised his hands, he whispered, "I sure as hell hope they don't figure out who we are."

"It don't matter none now," John said as he too raised his hands. "Our gooses are cooked anyway."

"At least Jodi got away," Jed said, resigned to the situation.

Jed always believed they'd get caught, sooner rather than later. They had sinned too much to be allowed such rewards. It was something he'd felt deep down inside for a long time. He knew his heart was black and sinful, and there was no penance for what they'd done. Maybe it was best this way. The running and killing would soon be over. He'd run enough for one lifetime.

They dodged bullets for years during the Civil War and for a half year as outlaws. Neither one expected to get caught without their guns in their hands, though. They would have preferred to go down fighting. But they weren't going to commit suicide either. There was no way for them to make it to the desk before the lawman shot them dead.

"I wonder what prison's like?" Jed asked.

"I reckon it won't be much different than slavery," John replied. "Now you're gonna get a taste of how I lived for most of my life."

CHAPTER 24

THE JAIL

JODI CAMPED OUT AT THE MEETING PLACE THEY ARRANGED to go to if they got split up. It was close enough to where the money was to be stashed to reach it quickly. It also was far enough away if someone saw them, they would never be able to find the money from the heist. The day slowly passed and, by nightfall, Jodi knew the last part of the robbery had gone wrong. If Jed and John weren't there by now, the authorities must have caught them.

She only hoped they didn't eventually discover who they were before she could come up with a plan to get them out of jail. Hell, first, she had to figure out where they were. If she went to a lawyer, it could take days to set bail. Of course, they had plenty of money, but putting up a large bail in a city where you just robbed a bank was risky business. She knew she didn't have days, though. It had to happen before the authorities discovered the men's identity.

If the local law enforcement found out they were part of Quantrill's Raiders, the Army would come and get them straight away. They'd be shot forthwith. Everywhere she looked in town, there were soldiers. She imagined some were there to control the crowd, which was becoming more unruly by the moment. Other revelers were with their families or girlfriends. Suddenly Jodi was jealous of a couple she saw walking down the street without a single care in the world. She was in love with Jed and enjoying a life of excitement and crime. It consumed her and there was nothing she could do about it. She prayed her plan for the day worked.

She had to get them back before they were carted off to who knows where. If the authorities forwarded them to some other jail, Jodi could lose track of them. Every day they were captive, they were closer to being discovered. Hopefully, the local marshal was lazy or still hadn't seen posters out on the pair of outlaws. They were wanted for just about every crime against humanity, even though Jodi knew it was due to no fault of their own. Nobody would believe her. Jed and John would be declared guilty before they even got to trial. War sure was hell.

It would be short and sweet if it was a court-martial, probably ending in a firing squad. Jodi had waited too long for the man she loved to come along. She wasn't going to let him escape her grasp without a fight. She would do everything in her power to see both Jed and John escaped wherever they were locked up.

She would have to go back into Austin and find out exactly what happened and if the sheriff had them locked up in town. She needed to see the exact location of the jail they occupied. Then, she had to find some weak points she would breach and get them out. Once they were out, she was confident Jed and John's escaping skills would take over like they did time and again during the war. All she wanted was to have Jed close by and safe again.

If there was a gun battle, she was all too aware both hardened Confederate soldiers would fight to the death. She pushed the possibility from her mind and was overwhelmed by the gut feeling they were alive and waiting for her to rescue them, just like in the fairy tales. Maybe she was a fool, but she knew any negative thinking could be disastrous. She had to think positive and straight. There was no time for distractions.

Looking back, they should have stayed in Mexico. They already had plenty of money for the next few years. They decided to rob the Austin bank just because they could. If only Jed and John had stuck to the plan, they would have enough money to forget it all and retire in the small Mexican town just far enough below the border to ward off nosy sheriffs and the Yankee Army. They didn't speak the language, but Jodi knew all three were capable. So, that was a hurdle they'd breach easily.

First, she had to devise a plan. Time was quickly running out. She buried the cash she stole and hid three thousand dollars in her boots just in case she had to bribe her way in or out of Austin.

She was determined to find them. Jodi saddled up Sandy and turned her toward Austin and town center where they had robbed the bank. She was dressed like any other cowgirl in these parts. She didn't look like she had thousands of dollars on her, nor did she look like a nun.

Nobody paid any mind to another cowboy or cowgirl in Austin. Jodi dressed herself down to make her look more like a man. Her long black hair was stuck down the back of her jacket. She certainly did ride a horse like a man and was strapped with a six-shooter and all. Still, she proceeded with care.

She found it strange the celebration was carrying on just like nothing happened. Her world felt like it was falling apart. She walked right by the entrance of the Austin bank they had robbed, but it was closed as tight as a drum for the holiday festivities. It looked as though it was never even robbed. It was getting dark, and the entire town appeared to be in the streets. She knew it was too early to read about the robbery in the newspapers. So, she turned to the next best thing and mingled through the crowd, listening for rumors and gossip of the bank robbery.

It didn't take her half an hour to run into a group of men and women talking on the subject. She closed in like any passerby looking for a good bit of gossip.

"I swear, they were two priests that robbed the bank," a tall, thin man with a wisp of hair said. "I saw the marshal take 'em to jail with my own eyes."

"But that's impossible," another spectator said. "Priests and preachers don't do such things."

"Are you hard of hearing? I tell ya I seen it with my own eyes," the first man insisted. "I even followed them to the jail. There must have been a hundred of us. How often do you see a pair of priests rob a bank, especially when one's Black?"

Jodi wondered if they continued with the ruse of being priests. It would be a stretch if they had their guns on them, but that didn't matter. All she needed to know was where they were locked up. A plan already began to formulate in her mind as she coyly approached one of the more gentlemanly men in the crowd.

"Could you please tell me where the marshal's office is, sir?" Jodi asked in her most mannerly voice.

The man glanced at her, took a double-take and said, "Why, yes, ma'am. We have two marshals' offices here in Austin. One is just around the block in the plaza where they're setting up the fireworks for tonight's display. Do you have a problem, young lady?"

"I need to report a horse theft," Jodi replied. "Somebody walked right off with my horse not twenty minutes ago. It happened right here in the middle of town."

"That's because all this riffraff is running the streets. Austin isn't normally like this. But the festivities have brought every thief and crook from a hundred miles to see what they can steal. Would you like for me to accompany you, ma'am?"

"That would be so kind of you, thank you," Jodi said. She smiled and batted her eyes.

The man escorted Jodi to the sheriff's office and knocked on the door. She immediately heard a chair scrape the floor and some grumbling. A man with a star opened the door. His frown turned into a smile when he saw the visitor was a young cowgirl with a well-known citizen.

"Is Sheriff Mosley about, Deputy?" the tall stranger asked.

"No, sir, Mr. Caldwell," the deputy replied. "He's one of the guests of honor at the celebration. He left me here to watch the dangerous criminals in the back cell." He craned his neck around and looked at the wind-up clock on the wall. "It'll start in less than an hour."

"This young lady has a problem I would like you to help her with, Harry. I must run now. Good luck, ma'am," the stranger said and scurried off.

"Howdy, ma'am. I'm Deputy Harry Wills. What can I do for you today?"

"Good morning, Deputy Wills," Jodi politely replied

as she proffered her hand and gave him her best smile. The deputy took it in his giant mitt, which dwarfed Jodi's. "I'm Josephina Wilson. Someone stole my horse right off the street. Right in front of the hardware store that's two blocks down. I've had Sandy since she was a colt, and it breaks my heart to think I've lost her."

"Today ain't a good day to leave property unattended, ma'am," Deputy Wills replied as he smoothed down his shirt with his hands and quickly brushed his hair out of his face. "I can make out a report, and if we run across any rustlers, we can check for the brand. Let me go and get a form we can fill out. I'll be right back."

Jodi knew she had to think fast. If she wasn't mistaken, Jed and John would be locked up at the end of the hall. She could almost see them from where she stood. If she could only let them know she was there, so they could get ready to run. She looked toward the room the deputy disappeared into and decided it was now or never. She shot down the hall like a bullet and nearly slipped as she headed around the bend. In front of her, Jed and John sat on bunks across from each other.

"Pssst. Get away from the wall and stay away. Hide behind your mattresses," she hissed, then turned and ran back down the hall arriving just as the deputy walked out the storeroom door.

"Here we are, ma'am," the deputy said as he studied the form. "Just fill this out, and I promise I'll do my best to find your horse. Just leave me a place to contact you, and I will follow it up; I swear."

He was doing his best to get the attention of the pretty, black-haired woman, but she had other plans. She had seen what she came here to see.

"I'll be danged," Jodi said as she stomped her foot and shook her head. "Now, that I think about it, I bet I left her in front of the hat shop. Let me go and check, and I'll be right back, Deputy."

Jodi turned and hurried out the door. She ran for two blocks, but with all the commotion nobody paid any attention. When she got to the three horses, she jumped on one and led the other two down an alley, at the end of the block from the jail. She looked at her watch and saw only ten minutes remained until the celebrations commenced.

She pulled the saddlebags off her horse and ran for the alley beside of the jailhouse. High up on the side of the building, there was a small square window with thick steel bars. Jodi looked around and saw a wooden crate. She dragged it below the window and climbed up, grabbing the bars and pulling her face up to the window. Her eyes peered into the dim room from the shadows of the alley. Jed's and John's eyes looked back questioningly.

"I'm gonna blow a hole in the wall, so get ready to take cover," Jodi said right before her grip gave out, and she dropped to the ground.

It was time to act. She dug a hole beside the thick jailhouse wall and shoved in two sticks of dynamite. Then she recalculated and added two more sticks and covered them up. Only the wicks showed. Then she backed into the corner in a deep shadow and did her best to hide. Hopefully, nobody would see her before the party began.

She began to doubt the amount of dynamite she placed against the wall as she lay there. Maybe she should have used all six sticks. She knew nothing about dynamite.

When the Fourth of July fireworks went off, and everybody looked up at the sky. Jodi lit the fuses, and they sparked to life. She ran for her life. The fuse was shorter than she thought, and the blast blew her off her feet. Her eagle feather flew from her hat, getting caught in the thermal current produced by the explosion. It swirled up and out of sight.

Jodi shook her head. Adobe dust flew from her hair and off her clothes. When she looked back, she was in shock. The entire side of the building was gone. Jed and John sat bewildered on the floor. Their faces were so black from the blast that it was hard to tell who was who. They still wore their robes, so they were black from the top of their heads to the tips of their feet.

"You liked to kill us," John said as he staggered out of the demolished building with Jed right behind.

You could see all the way in to where the deputy was sitting. Lucky for him, he ran outside the moment the fireworks went off. He got blown off the front porch and sat covered in dust in the middle of the street. When Jodi turned to run for the horses, he was still shaking his head, trying to clear the fog.

The three ran down the block for the horses. They didn't have to rush, though. The only people who noticed the jail had been blown up were the folks standing next to it. The rest were still staring at the sky and the cacophony of fireworks. They removed their priestly garb, mounted their horses and ran south for their lives.

WHEN THEY REACHED THE EDGE OF TOWN, THEY REALIZED there still was an immense number of people streaming into Austin. Many saw the fireworks from afar, but there were still the promised festivities along with the carnival and freak show. They slowed their horses to a trot. Jed and John pulled off their bandanas, soaked them in water from their canteens, and wiped the dust and dirt from their faces and eyes.

"You nearly brought the building down," Jed said as he spat dirt. "How much dynamite did you use?"

"I was going to use two sticks, but I used four on second thought." Jodi grinned. "I gotcha out, though, didn't I."

"I don't know who's crazier — you or us." John chuckled. "It was brave of you to break us out."

"If it wasn't for the Fourth of July festivities, I doubt I'd have had any idea how to bust you free," Jodi said. "We got away again by using the masses. I have Sandy and two more horses waiting a few hours away. I've got three thousand dollars on me, so we have plenty of money. I suppose it's time to head back to Mexico. No Texas city lawmen or posse will chase us that far, even if they hail from Austin. Did they figure out who you are? What'd they say about your priestly robes?"

"Oh, the sheriff was a clever old fella." John chuckled. Now that he was free again, he felt great. "He thought the robes were funny as hell and made us keep 'em on 'til we went before the judge. He said his honor would enjoy the humor. He ain't gonna like it when we ain't there to show him."

"I believe they're gonna be more upset with Jodi destroying the building," Jed said. "I think we best keep riding for a few days, if not a week. I doubt they take kindly to all we've done there."

"Nobody will link a Black and a White bank robber, dressed like priests, with Quantrill's Raiders," John said. "At least not until the sheriff gets back to work and studies his wanted posters. We know there's one on Jed and me. We done seen it. There's a reward, too."

"Why didn't you tell me?" Jodi asked, surprised and a little hurt. "How long have you known?"

"We didn't know if we could trust you with our lives yet," Jed said and hesitated like he was still deciding. "Now we do. When a man has money on his head, sometimes his friends change. We meant no offense. We've been running from a lot of demons for a long time. We've come to distrust anyone we don't know."

"How much money was in the two sacks you got away with?" John asked.

"I don't know," Jodi said. "I never counted it. But all the bills were large denominations and wrapped up and stamped. I'd say in one bag; we got more than we did in all four from the last bank. There must have been a million dollars in that safe with the gold and all."

It began to sting Jed's pride. He and John got greedy, and it nearly cost them their freedom. Jodi wasn't much bigger than a corn nugget, but she was as smart as a whip. He never saw anybody plan like her, nor had John.

"I reckon we should've listened to ya," Jed said. "We got crazy seeing all that gold. It was like it hit us with a fever."

"Just because she's a woman sure don't mean she's dumb." John chuckled. "We've learned our lesson."

Jodi rolled her eyes in disbelief. "How much longer did you stay after I left?"

"Maybe fifteen minutes, but it could have been more," John said.

"The sheriff said he was watching us for five minutes at the door. He was trying to make out what two priests were doing in the bank. He claimed as soon as he saw the CLOSED sign in the window in the middle of the day, he knew something was amiss," Jed admitted. "I reckon we overstayed our visit by double what you said."

"Next time, we should go when the bank is about to close," Jodi said as the gears began to grind in the brain again. "Then it won't seem strange if the CLOSED sign is out."

"Hold on a minute," Jed said as he pulled to a stop. "How about we get away from the posse we're gonna have on our asses right now. Once we're free, we can talk about if we carry on robbin' banks or not."

Jodi was surprised. Only a day ago she was telling herself they should have quit. Now, she was sure she could plan another one that would be totally safe.

"Really?" Jodi asked. "No more banks?"

"John and I got to talking while we were locked up and waiting on the Army to show up. We decided we needed to change our lives from now on."

"I feel like I'm in one of those spinning doors we saw in Austin," John said. "You know, the ones that go round and round. At this point, I don't know what I am. Free, enslaved, or imprisoned. It's like I was in one of those swinging doors; every time I walk through, my situation changes."

"And?" Jodi asked.

Her brow furrowed and her eyes narrowed. She held her breath. Were they going to leave her after all they've done? She looked from John to Jed. She didn't know what she would do if Jed decided to leave her now that she felt he had growing feelings for her.

"You look like you been shot at and missed and shit at and hit." John laughed.

"We decided no more robbing banks, Jodi, and that's the last of it," Jed said. "We're gonna go find us a train to rob."

"But nobody's ever robbed a train!" Jodi replied as she breathed a deep sigh of relief.

"Exactly," Jed said. "Since nobody's done it, we could rob three or four before they got the hang of catching train robbers. We just need to figure out how to stop the train and not get shot by the passengers and the engineer. That's where you come in, darlin'."

Again, Jed used the endearment she loved. She wondered if he did it to get her to do what he wanted or if he really meant it.

Why do men have to be so complicated all the time?

Jodi hadn't hidden how she felt but getting information from Jed was like pulling teeth from a rattlesnake.

"Let me think on it a while, honey," Jodi replied, baiting Jed. "Where is the closest train around here anyway?"

"I ain't even sure if there are trains in Texas yet," John

said. "But if we can't find a train, we can find a steamboat. They be full of money from the casinos onboard."

"Yeah, steamboats run from Galveston down to the border to ship cotton," Jodi said. "Hmmm. Trains and steamboats. I reckon banks ain't the only way to go."

"If we beat Jesse and Frank to robbing trains, they ain't gonna like it one bit," Jed said, chuckling.

"I'm beginning to like the idea already." John smiled. "When all is said and done, I reckon I like stealing money from rich White folks more than I like shootin' 'em."

A LOOK AT BOOK TWO:
UNWANTED REUNION

They escaped the war…now the whole world wants them dead.

Jed Coal and John Noland deserted Quantrill's Raiders with blood on their hands and a price on their heads. The Union wants them hanged, the Confederacy wants them shot, and nearly every lawman in the West is on their trail. Jodi Goodnight never meant to be an outlaw—but one violent mistake forced her into a life on the run. Teaming up with two ex-Raiders seemed reckless, but it may be her only way out.

South of the border, the trio plots a bold heist aboard the *Texas Belle*, a glittering casino riverboat out of Galveston. But with Jesse and Frank James back in the picture—and Sgt. Rooster Beastly hunting them down—the score could cost them everything.

Forced into crime by fate, driven by desperation, they must decide how far they'll go to escape the past that refuses to die.

Will they burn out in a blaze of glory—or carve out a place in a world that never wanted them to survive?

AVAILABLE JULY 2025

ABOUT THE AUTHOR

 Born in 1886 in Southern Ohio, Ash Lingam grew crops, raised cattle, and doted on the young boy. Ash's family was among the early settlers in pre-Revolutionary America. He has traced his lineage back to around 1746 when his ancestors immigrated from Europe to the aspiring American Colonies.

A retired marketing executive, Ash devotes his spare time to training police dogs and writing novels. He has found his niche in the Western, historical fiction, and adventure genres. With his vast vault of experience, he never runs out of sources for new stories. He has lived in eleven different countries and worked in a total of forty-six to date, Ash has written approximately 130 novels, short stories, and poems. More than one hundred of his eclectic titles help the American frontier come alive for his readers.

https://www.ashlingam.com/